# WARLORD
## *of the* GENJI

# Dale Carlson

# WARLORD
of the GENJI

illustrated by John Gretzer

ATHENEUM 1970 NEW YORK

For Al Carlson

# Contents

# Foreword

From the tenth century until a time near the end of the twelfth century, the noble Fujiwara clan reigned supreme over the great Golden Heian Period in Japanese history. The secret of their glory lay in their knowledge that the power of the mind is greater than that of the sword. They knew also that it was better to rule in the name of the emperor than to secure the throne for themselves. They served as principal advisors to the throne, supplied the imperial family with wives, and became regents to the young emperors, who were usually Fujiwara grandsons. In return for their power, the Fujiwaras gave to Japan a golden age of culture, created an orderly government, and maintained peace.

But their age of glory passed, and the Fujiwaras grew corrupt. To support their luxurious court life they needed huge sums of money. To collect their enormous taxes and to maintain law and order, the Fujiwaras relied on the two greatest warrior clans, the Heike and the Genji. Living close to the land and surrounded by professional soldiers, the warrior clans became more and more powerful while the luxury-loving Fujiwara government grew weaker.

As the Fujiwara government spent more and more money on the court, it gave less and less to the powerful temples of Mt. Hiei and Nara. Thousands of angry monks swooped down to launch battles in Kyoto. It was necessary to call the warrior clans into the capital to restore order. To Kiyomori of the Heike and Tameyoshi of the Genji fell the task of suppressing the monks and protecting the throne.

It was Kiyomori of the Heike who finally stopped the monk warfare. Then came two wars with the Genji over who was to be emperor. Twice Kiyomori won, and he put Goshirakawa of the Fujiwara on the throne. Kiyomori also outlawed the Genji and restored peace to Kyoto—until the Genji rose again under their chieftain Yoritomo and his younger brother and greatest warlord, Yoshitsune of the Genji.

In any event, the courtly Fujiwaras were doomed. The warrior class had come into power, to rule Japan and its puppet emperors under a military dictatorship until the last half of the nineteenth century, when the Emperor Meiji returned the power to the throne. So much for the historical background of a story that was a legend even before it was over.

# WARLORD
## *of the* GENJI

# The Demons of Kurama Mountain

A silent figure wrapped in a long gray cloak waited in the dark shadow of a mountain shrine. He stood motionless, patient as an ancient statue of Buddha, his glance fastened on the monastery below. He listened and waited in a stillness that was broken only by the rustling of bamboo grass or the sudden call of a cuckoo. It was midnight, the Hour of the Rat.

A slim boy slid open an outer screen of the monastery, glanced up from the long, open veranda, paused for a moment by the railing, then vaulted to the ground, and glided off with the swiftness of a mountain deer.

"Yoshitsune!"

At the sound of the low voice, the young man sped into the black shadows of the pine forest and waited. The cloaked figure followed noiselessly.

"I did not mean to startle you," he said.

Yoshitsune smiled. "Konnomaru! Come, I'm later than last night. The others will be waiting."

Konnomaru's stern face softened with affection and amusement. "We have all waited a long time, hiding in these hills. We can wait a little longer."

3

"I have finished waiting, Konnomaru," Yoshitsune said impatiently.

In sudden obedience, Konnomaru bowed. "Yes, master."

The two hurried down into the darkness of the valley. From the distance came the tolling of the temple bell.

People said that winged demons—the Tengu—haunted the crags and forests of Kurama Mountain and played pranks in the mountain's steep valleys. On stormy nights, the villagers crouched in their bamboo huts, whispering in terror that the flying Tengu, with their beaked noses and claws of a tiger, were holding their revels. Few had seen the Tengu, for to spy on them meant death. But the people of Kurama Mountain knew who unleashed the torrents that washed away rice paddies; who hurled rocks down the mountainside; who lit the fires on the highest peaks. Lately, the demons of Kurama Mountain had been worse than ever before. Meetings of strange, masked figures were known to take place in a valley of Kurama Mountain.

There were two possible ways for Yoshitsune and Konnomaru to descend into the valley. Most of Kurama Mountain was covered with Buddhist monasteries. They could pass through these, and usually that was what they did. The other way was down the dangerous valley wall.

Yoshitsune moved in the direction of the steep cliffs. Konnomaru's hand held him back.

"If you should slip on the rocks, what then?"

"I should die," replied Yoshitsune in a steady voice. "But quick death of the body is better than slow death of the heart. And I keep worrying about the monastery guards. If they should see me, if I am caught . . ." His voice grew mischievous. "And where the Tengu go, I can go."

He sped off into the thicket, and as the wisps of the spring night haze hid him from view, Konnomaru hurried to follow. They came to where the pine trees gripped a ledge of stone, and Yoshitsune stared down the steep rock face. His darting glance missed nothing. Quickly he spied a way and leaped down to the branches of a tree a few feet below the edge.

"Come, follow me. It is not difficult."

Konnomaru grasped some shrubs and lowered himself slowly into the tree.

"Yoshitsune! Look below!"

Down the steep mountainside a waterfall roared into a foaming pool and sprayed high fans of water into the air.

Yoshitsune's soft laughter accepted the challenge. He dropped to the lowest branch of the tree and his feet searched for a hold in the rock.

"Follow me," he murmured.

A pale moonlight flooded the face of the valley wall. From below, silent figures with glittering swords at their sides watched with pride and adoration the agile form gliding from boulder to boulder, leaping from tree to tree. Down he swung toward the rock-strewn valley.

"Take care," called Konnomaru.

"You needn't worry about me," Yoshitsune shouted back.

"You have become like a mountain monkey."

The figure paused for a moment. He was not tall, but there was great strength in his wiry body. His thinness and the light, tattered tunic, which was all he wore, showed how little care he had been given at the monastery. His dignity under hardship, the proud nobility of his bearing, and his wildly changeable moods all upset the monks. So did the rumors of his true identity. And though the monks punished him cruelly, they could not control his fiery temper or stubborn silences. Nor had they been able to turn him into a quiet and proper novice of the priesthood. Yoshitsune was bored by the long hours of Buddhist prayers and meditation. He often escaped from the lecture hall to walk by himself the wide cloister corridors or to closet himself in his cell and think his own thoughts.

He had been happiest during the periods of training in arms.

Kurama monastery, like the other nearby monasteries, trained its monks to fight in order to protect their rights and guard their huge estates. The three thousand warrior-priests, the *yamabushi*, were led by abbots, many of whom were imperial princes in holy orders and wielded great influence in the capital city of Kyoto.

As Yoshitsune continued his climb down the steep mountain wall, he thought how grateful he was to the monks for his warrior training. Once he had played at the exercises as fun. Now he practiced seriously. He was even learning to control his temper. He knew that the Sojo, his superior, had noticed the change in him. Did the Sojo think, Yoshitsune wondered, that his new seriousness was due to the monastery's training? Or did his superior know the truth—that Yoshitsune had discovered what had been hidden from him for so long.

The sudden appearance of Konnomaru, and then the meetings of the Tengu in the valley below, had caused the change. From them he had learned who he was. He was their chieftain, the son of Yoshitomo of the great warrior clan of the Genji. And he was a prisoner of Kiyomori of the now victorious rival clan of the Heike. He learned also from the Tengu of his father's swift and snowy death, of the exile of his elder brother, of his scattered clan hiding in the mountains, waiting for their leader, for Yoshitsune. True, his elder brother Yoritomo was the rightful clan chieftain. But for the time being, Yoritomo was in captivity and was powerless. Yoshitsune knew what he had to do, and he was aware of the dangers.

One more moment on the cliff, and then he was among the boulders of the valley. The wind sang in the ravines, and the silent figures before him tensed. Quickly they lit the bamboo flares and rose as Yoshitsune appeared before them.

"My lord!"

"Well done!"

Yoshitsune smiled at the faces of his followers. Two were newly arrived and had not been at the earlier meetings.

"Goro," Konnomaru greeted one of them as he moved into the torchlight. "It is good to see you here. Did you have much difficulty? Kawata, you came, too. What news from the east?"

The two men bowed to Yoshitsune, who leaned forward eagerly to hear the news they brought. The two had traveled from the far eastern mountains of Japan where, in the home of Tokimasa of the Hojo, cousin clan to the enemy Heike, Yoritomo had been held prisoner since he was fourteen. It was now 1175. Yoshitsune was sixteen, Yoritomo twenty-nine. The time was ripe to raise the white banner of the Genji against the red banner of the Heike.

"I have interesting news this time, Konnomaru," said Goro. There was a glint of humor in his eyes. "Yoritomo has eloped with Tokimasa's daughter."

Yoshitsune was amused to see the old retainer Adachi spit at the idea of Yoritomo marrying the daughter of the enemy.

"Yoritomo is wise," Goro continued. "He always knows the right thing to do. Masako is a remarkable girl. But more important, the situation in the east is changing. Yoritomo has made powerful friends. The leading families in the east may be Heike, but they are not at all sympathetic with their cousins here in the capital. They despise the elegance of the imperial court and the soft court ways of their clansmen, who have forgotten they are warrior lords. Their interest is in the land, not in court life. Little by little, Yoritomo has won them over. Their sympathy is with the Genji now. And when the time comes . . ."

"The time is now," said Yoshitsune suddenly.

"Yoritomo says we must be patient," Goro replied. "We must wait until the time is a little more ripe."

Kawata said, "There are rumors that all is not well between ex-Emperor Goshirakawa and Kiyomori. If they are busy fighting each other, it might be a perfect time for us to attack."

"Patience . . . might . . . if," muttered Yoshitsune. "The time is near when I am to take my vows. I will have none of that. If you will not help me now, I will escape by myself."

"Yoritomo has made plans," said Goro.

"I am sure my brother is very wise. But his subtle ways are different from mine," said Yoshitsune.

"He has accomplished much," said Konnomaru quietly.

"True," answered Yoshitsune. "But I am not so patient. For me the time is now."

"It will be dangerous without the proper arrangements," said Goro.

Yoshitsune glared at the small band. Though still in his teens, he understood things quickly and his decisions were sure and immediate. "This arguing is useless," he said. "It is one month until the festival, and the mountain will be crowded with pilgrims."

Konnomaru understood. "With so many people about, it might be a long time before they noticed your absence."

"The day of the procession it shall be," whispered Yoshitsune, and the corners of his mouth hardened in defiance.

The rest of the night was spent making plans for Yoshitsune's escape.

"Enough now," said Konnomaru finally. "Yoshitsune must get back. It is already the Hour of the Tiger."

The morning haze rose like steam from the mountain. It was not yet light and the stillness was dreamlike. Yoshitsune rose to go. After exchanging glances with the members of the small group, he made his way back up the mountain. Over a tall pine tree, a trail of wisteria blossoms quivered, shaken by a sudden gust of wind. In the stillness, Yoshitsune could feel excitement bursting within him.

When Yoshitsune returned to the monastery he paused at the Great Southern Gate and stared up at the forbidding statues of the Nio, twin guardians of Buddhism. Their scowling faces and bulging eyes kept evil from the temple. He went in, past the large bell, the tall, narrow pagoda, and the Great Buddha Hall, where flickering candles burned before the Amida Buddha and the Bodhisattvas. There was a faint fragrance of burning incense in the morning air. He moved on toward the hall of meditation.

On the veranda sat an upright, thoughtful figure, legs crossed beneath him, chin resting on his hand. Outlined against the cool and empty hall, the figure might have been a carved image. It was the Sojo, Yoshitsune's superior.

The low voice of the Sojo called his name. When Yoshitsune turned, the Sojo smoothed the purple robes of his high office and motioned him near. Yoshitsune mounted the wooden steps, crossed the polished wood floor of the veranda, and seated himself by the side of the Sojo.

*"Ohayo gozaimasu,"* he said warily. "Good morning."

The Sojo clapped his hands and a servant appeared carrying a lacquer tray. On the tray were two bowls of rice, two bowls for tea, and a small pot.

"You will breakfast with me." It was not a question.

Yoshitsune bowed his thanks. It was better food than he would have received in the novice's dining hall.

"I wish to speak about your mother," said the Sojo.

Yoshitsune stiffened. He remained silent.

Then he burst out, "Why do you choose to speak of my mother?"

The Sojo handed him a small case of crimson brocade and a letter. In the case was a silver image.

"The image belonged to your father."

Yoshitsune drew a sharp breath and quickly hid the image in his sleeve.

"I have not read it, of course," said the Sojo, "but I can tell you what is in the letter. It may surprise you to know that I have visited your mother."

Yoshitsune was not altogether surprised. He knew that many of the powerful monasteries were in secret sympathy with the Genji. What was surprising was that anyone at all was permitted to visit the beautiful Tokiwa.

"I bribed the porter and slipped in secretly," said the Sojo in answer to Yoshitsune's unasked question.

"How is she?" His voice betrayed a sudden rush of emotion.

"She is worried. She hears rumors about you. She prays night and day that you will study hard and take your vows. I did my best to soothe her. She has had a very hard time."

Yoshitsune's mouth tightened. "What are these rumors you speak of?"

"You know very well." The Sojo's eyes were steady.

"And you know that what my mother asks is impossible."

"She wishes only to see her sons live in peace. She has lived through two clan wars and seen her family and husband live and die in bloodshed. I speak to you like this because I have seen that you have discovered who and what you are."

So the Sojo knew that Yoshitsune had found out the truth about himself and no longer trusted him to go on quietly as before. "Do you agree with my mother's wishes?" Yoshitsune asked.

"I will tell you something you may not know," said the Sojo. "After the Hogen and Heiji wars, more than fifteen years ago . . ."

"The Heike soldiers killed my father at Gojo Bridge. I know."

"Kiyomori of the Heike held the lives of your mother and four young children in the palm of his hand. Your mother was, is, beautiful, and when she begged Kiyomori to spare you, he agreed. Yoritomo, your half-brother, was sent east; and you, Otowaka, and Imawaka were destined to take holy orders. The others have done so. And you?"

Yoshitsune remained silent. So far he had learned nothing he had not already known.

"Do you know what your mother did to safeguard your lives?" pursued the Sojo. "She gave herself to Kiyomori, your father's greatest enemy. And later, when Kiyomori tired of her, he thoughtfully married her to a half-idiotic clansman. Kiyomori still protects her from the vengeance of the rest of the Heike, but her life is a sorrowful one."

"Why do you tell me these things?" The shock and agony he felt echoed in Yoshitsune's voice. He had not known of his mother's relationship to Kiyomori.

"So that you do not add to her suffering," said the Sojo.

# Escape from Kurama

The sun rose over the Eastern Hills, and thousands of lamps still glimmered in the early dawn. The sounds of mountain birds and the notes of a flute mingled with the distant roar of hurrying waters.

It was the last day of the festival. The mountain was swarming with pilgrims. As the sun rose higher the mist cleared and the day grew sparkling and warm. Crowds surged up the paths, spilling over into the surrounding woods. Ox-drawn carriages, colorfully draped, carried persons of quality as far as the foothills, where they had to dismount. There, ladies, who never allowed themselves to be seen in public, were provided with curtained litters. The gentlemen, with their outriders, went on horseback. Peasants from faraway provinces with their wives and children; queer wild men with bare feet and begging bowls; thousands of people from the capital; all created a spectacle of color and confusion.

The novices were gathered in a room behind the dance stage preparing for the ritual sacred dances. From time to time, one of them slid open the outer screen and peered out.

"Look! The whole mountain looks like a giant ant hill."

"See, the court nobles have arrived. What splendid cloaks and trousers they wear!"

"There is the carriage of the minister of the left. I know the livery his attendants wear."

Only Yoshitsune, dressed in purple trousers and scarlet tunic, his hair done in an elaborate knot before the ceremony of the shaving of the head, sat quietly apart.

A black-robed monk of low rank entered the room to warn them that the procession was about to begin. Excitedly, the novices gave last minute tugs on their trouser sashes and straightened their tunics.

The procession began, cutting its own path through the crowds. First came the musicians, sounding bells and gongs; then the high priests in their red and purple robes, and finally the novices who were to take part later in the sacred dramas. The procession wound around the mountain, from shrine to shrine, temple to temple, for four hours. Exhausted, people plumped themselves down where they stood and opened lunch boxes and lit bonfires. Vendors sold balls of rice sweetened with bean paste, and pickles and other delicacies.

Then it was time for the sacred dramas and the dancing and the musical concerts. The crowds pushed this way and that, trying not to miss any of it.

As Yoshitsune marched in the procession with the others an occasional gleam of recognition came into his eyes. Here and there he saw through the disguise of a shabby pilgrim, or a begging monk, or a vendor of bamboo baskets. His Genji Tengu were there! All was going as planned.

As the procession broke up the crowds became more disorderly than ever. Suddenly a gray summer cloak was thrown over Yoshitsune to hide his scarlet tunic.

"Now, my lord!"

"Is that you, Konnomaru?" whispered Yoshitsune, his voice choked with excitement.

"Yes—hurry!"

Yoshitsune and Konnomaru lost no time in milling with the crowd. A minute later they were completely hidden by two or three beggars, a few rather fierce-looking pilgrims, and a vendor who caused havoc with his bamboo baskets. Under cover of this strange shield, Konnomaru hurried Yoshitsune toward the valley where they held their nightly meetings.

Soon a cry went up among the crowds. At one of the road barriers, a Heike guard had been killed. People shuddered.

"Careful! The Tengu demons are angry again."

From his safe hiding place in the valley, Yoshitsune thought of the great Kiyomori.

"Does he know yet that I am free?" Yoshitsune wondered, and then exultantly, "And that my escape is the first step toward his downfall?"

Simply clad in the white silken kimono of his nightdress, Kiyomori of the Heike paced the wide, empty corridors of his mansion at Rokuhara far into the night. He paused on the veranda overlooking his beautiful garden. A sudden gust of wind carried the faint scent of wisteria, and flecks of moonlight played in the stream. Of all the seasons, early summer gave him most pleasure. As the fireflies darted where the stream played on the rocks, Kiyomori sighed and remembered a time when such beauty had not been part of his Japanese warrior's life.

Kiyomori stared at the sky. A thread of cloud floated across the moon, and Kiyomori shivered. The Hour of the Ox. It was three hours before the sun would rise, but he had no wish to go to bed.

The sound of a commotion reached him, and he turned to see the police commissioner hurriedly striding along the gallery. His son Shigemori was not far behind.

"Well, what is it?" Kiyomori asked.

The police commissioner bowed nervously and blurted out, "Yoshitsune has escaped." He fumbled for words, horrified at his own news. "I . . . we . . . everything possible is being done."

"You will find him." Kiyomori's voice was harsh. "Immediately. Use whatever help you need. He has to be brought back."

"*Hai*. Yes, my lord." The police commissioner's words were without conviction.

"Go now," Kiyomori commanded. "Suspect everyone."

Bowing and scraping his feet, the commissioner withdrew.

Shigemori remained, standing quietly. He had been on duty at the court and was still in his court robes. His long trousers trailed gracefully behind him, and the long brocaded sleeves of his court robes fell in perfect folds. The high black silk hat still rose above his sensitive face.

"Father . . ."

Kiyomori was silent, leaning on the balustrade.

"Are you blaming me?" Shigemori's voice was soft and even.

"You begged for his life," Kiyomori replied.

"So did we all, your stepmother, your brother, and I. There had been so much bloodshed. You, too, had had enough, or you would not have spared Yoshitomo's sons."

Neither of them mentioned the power of Tokiwa's beauty.

Kiyomori's voice was angry. "Yes, I spared them. It was the most deadly mistake I have ever made. You do not realize what it will mean. You do not see far enough. But I see. And I tell you I should never have let them live."

There would be trouble soon, Kiyomori knew. Not everyone was pleased with the way he had managed things. And rumors had reached him that the Genji were not altogether crushed, that they were gathering forces to again challenge the Heike. The rumors came mostly from Kurama Mountain, coupled with strange stories of the Tengu. The escape at such a time, obviously well-planned, was unfortunate.

"Yes," Kiyomori continued. "It was all very well to spare their lives. But fifteen years have passed, and they are not children now. They are old enough to start another civil war."

He paused, and his voice sounded tired.

"I have had enough of wars, Shigemori, enough of court intrigues and monkish battles."

He turned from the railing, a spray of blossoms in his hand. Grinding the petals in his fingers, he glanced down.

"If it is not too late, if it is not too late to catch Yoshitsune, I shall order the death of every Genji who has taken part in his escape."

"And the others? The other sons?"

"Two have already taken their vows for the priesthood. They are harmless. Yoritomo is well guarded in the east. But Yoshitsune and his followers . . . I shall hang them."

"He is not much more than a child."

"Are you saying I have no feelings? Think then, if I spare that child, as you call him—though he is no child anymore—I shall expose us all to endless threats and to war."

"I understand," said Shigemori sorrowfully. "I shall not bring up the matter again."

In the hills west of Kurama Mountain the Kamo River began its course, running directly south between Mount Hiei and Mount Atago into the capital. South of the capital, it was joined by the Katsura River, and the two together became the Yodo River, which flowed to Naniwa on the Inland Sea.

"As it is the most obvious route, it will be the least expected," said Konnomaru. "We shall follow the course of the Kamo River directly to the capital."

"Kyoto!" Goro drew his breath sharply. "Right under Kiyomori's nose. You cannot mean it."

"It is there that everything is to be arranged."

"But the roads will be blocked and the city gates guarded. No doubt they are searching every house by now."

"It will still be far easier to hide Yoshitsune in the crowds of the capital than risk the Heike warriors who swarm the countryside. Later, when they find we are not in the hills, they will search harder in Kyoto. Then it will be time for us to make our way east."

The others shook their heads doubtfully.

"Don't worry. It has all been planned. Our friends wait for us now in Kyoto."

"Konnomaru is right," said Yoshitsune sharply.

In his bearing and the tone of his voice were already the qualities that make men follow and obey. The arguing ceased.

"In any case," his voice was soft now, "it may be the last chance I shall have to see my mother."

Konnomaru rested his hand lightly on the young man's shoulder. "I understand what you feel. But nothing could be more dangerous. Of all, she will be the most closely watched."

Yoshitsune rose and moved toward the opening of the cave in which they had been hiding, waiting for nightfall. His steps were soundless, and treading his way carefully among the trailing vines, he sat by the side of the mountain stream.

"Listen, Konnomaru. The sounds of the summer cicada fill the air. The cicada knows neither spring nor fall. His season is short, but filled with warmth and beauty. He does not live long, but he lives fully."

The stern lines of Konnomaru's face softened. "Do you have such thoughts indeed?"

Yoshitsune smiled. "You have been a good friend. I thank you," he said simply.

Late that night a small band of drunken musicians, after much noisy arguing and playing of their flutes and zitherns, were permitted entrance at the north gate of the capital. A guard accompanied them part way, and seeing that they were headed for the gay quarters, laughed and returned to his post.

# The Gay Quarters

Once the guard was behind them, the behavior of the musicians changed. They crept as quietly and quickly as possible along the willow-fringed Kamo River on the eastern edge of the city. When they came to Gojo Bridge they stopped.

"The marketplace is just here on Fifth Avenue," whispered old Adachi.

"Shall I be able to get in touch with you?" Konnomaru shifted his cloak to cover the lower part of his face.

"No. We cannot remain in Kyoto. Our faces are too well known. I shall inform our friends that you have arrived safely and leave immediately," said Adachi.

"Where shall we meet again?" asked Konnomaru.

"In the east."

Goro nodded. "I must return to Izu and bring news to Yoritomo of what has happened."

"Goodby. Good luck." Kawata of the Tengu smiled. "Take good care of the young master—he is wild like the mountain deer."

Yoshitsune stood a little way off by the water, staring at the great Gojo Bridge, which spanned the Kamo, linking the capital

19

on its eastern side with the Eastern Hills. On that bridge his father had died. Beyond it was Kiyomori's mansion Rokuhara. His enemy was close.

The small band waited respectfully until Yoshitsune came near. He gazed at each in turn. "I thank you for your help," he said, bowing courteously.

In a moment the three men had vanished into the shadows of a nearby alley.

"Come."

Yoshitsune followed Konnomaru farther down the river until they reached the section known as Horikawa, the gay quarters of Kyoto. Here courtiers, samurai, and some of the wealthier merchants came for the refined entertainments of the trained geisha or for coarser pleasures. Wooden houses with sliding rice paper doors fronted the tiny, narrow streets. Before them, gay paper lanterns and colored strips of cloth proclaimed each establishment's name.

Near the canal the willows bent gently to the water. Sounds of a flute and the plucked notes of a koto mingled with the warm fragrance of the summer night. The two turned into a side street and stopped in front of a small house. Yoshitsune heard laughter within.

The door was swiftly slid open at Konnomaru's knock.

"Ah, it is you," said the woman who opened the door. "*Irashaimase*. You are welcome. All is ready. We have been waiting for you."

They were led along the outer veranda to a room in the back of the house, overlooking a small garden.

"Please excuse this humble room. I will tell Sochi you are here."

The woman scurried out.

"How long shall we be here?" Yoshitsune asked.

"It depends on what happens. Probably, we shall not make the journey east until fall. We cannot hope to pass the road barriers now. It was not difficult to enter the city. It will be nearly impossible to get out. We must wait until the soldiers stop searching the mountains. And for the time being you will be safe enough in this room."

"In this room?" questioned Yoshitsune.

"You must not leave it," said Konnomaru carefully. "Sochi, it is good to see you."

An old man whose eyes twinkled in his wrinkled face had entered.

"So this is he." A pleased chuckle lightened the room as much as the candle he carried. "I am most happy that you consider me worthy of serving you. Please make my home yours."

He bowed deeply to Yoshitsune, then clapped his hands.

Rice wine and a bowl of fresh fruit were brought. Yoshitsune listened as Sochi and Konnomaru exchanged political views far into the night. Sochi, once a loyal retainer in the house of Yoshitomo, Yoshitsune's father, was still courageously serving the interests of the Genji in whatever way he could. From his careful glance, Yoshitsune knew that Sochi was measuring him against his father. When a gleam of satisfaction lit the old man's eyes, Yoshitsune was pleased.

Finally, the older men withdrew and a little maid entered the room to arrange the bedclothes.

She was dressed in a brightly colored kimono and her hair fell in silky lengths to her shoulders. She looked about eight years old.

Yoshitsune watched her from the corner of his eye as she deftly pulled the quilts and pillows into place on the floor. She flitted about the room, swift as a small bird.

"Are you . . . are you a dancing girl?" His curiosity had gotten the better of him.

The child looked up, surprised. Then she giggled. "Surely you must know a dancing girl when you see one." Gracefully she fluttered the sleeves of her flowered kimono.

"No . . . I . . . that is . . ." Yoshitsune was learning to command grown men, to accept their homage with dignity. Yet this mere wisp of a girl confused him. He cleared his throat. "I have just come from the country."

"Oh, I know who you are," she whispered in conspiracy. Then, coolly, "If you wish, I will call one of the dancing girls. I am Sochi's granddaughter. My name is Nobuko."

As Yoshitsune drew nearer the lamp, the child fell silent. She blushed prettily and lowered her eyes. Yoshitsune smiled.

"Come closer."

Nobuko crept to his feet.

"Now I would say that you are a person one can trust."

"Oh, yes," breathed Nobuko.

"Do you know the city well?"

She nodded. "I often have to go on errands."

"Good. You shall be my guide. Not a word to anyone. I am not even supposed to poke my nose out of this room."

Nobuko nodded delightedly. "I shall come back in the morning."

"Sleep well," said Yoshitsune.

Twelfth century Kyoto resembled nothing so much as a grand checkerboard. There were nine major avenues running east and west and nine running north and south. The area between First Avenue and Second Avenue, at the northern end of the city, was larger than the area between any of the other streets, and directly in the center of this space, was the Imperial Palace, with its many halls of residence, ceremonial halls, ministries, and gardens. In the rest of the city, each big square was divided up and space awarded according to rank. While the nobles had lovely mansions, the houses of the poor were so crowded together it was impossible to tell where one left off and the next began.

In the jostling crowds of the marketplace no one paid any

attention to a figure in torn trousers and straw sandals. The rag tied around his head covered the lower part of his face, and only the fine, dark eyes might have betrayed him had someone looked closely. At his side trotted a little girl more ragged than the urchins who played under the great Rashomon Gate. Together they pushed among the stalls, inspecting the bamboo wares, dyed cloth, and all the trinkets and foodstuffs on display.

"Hungry?"

The child smiled.

Passing under the *noren,* the warm curtain of blue cloth that hung at the entrance of a booth, they bought some rice balls wrapped in seaweed and some balls with dried fish in the middle. They ate as they walked on. Fourth and Fifth Avenues contained better shops, and the two peered at the silks and brocades, the gilded lacquerware, the woven cricket cages, and an artisan who was handpainting summer fans.

"I know a lovely place," said the girl.

Yoshitsune followed. He wanted to know every inch of the city. He would need such knowledge later.

On East Third Avenue stood the Cloister Palace where retired emperors lived. Often, as with Goshirakawa, an emperor retired in order not to be bothered with court etiquette. Nevertheless, he continued to run the political life of the country. Ex-Emperor Goshirakawa's palace not only rivaled the Imperial Palace as a seat of government, but also as the leader of fashion and gaiety. In its spacious rooms and splendid gardens, poetry contests and moon viewing parties, games of football, and dancing exhibitions amused the elegant courtiers.

As they neared the front gates, Yoshitsune and Nobuko saw countless ox-carts and carriages awaiting their owners.

"This way," called Nobuko.

She darted around to a side hedge where a careless gardener had neglected to cover a gap. Together they peered through the hole. The warm fragrance of summer grass filled the air. They could see only part of the garden at the side of Goshirakawa's splendid mansion.

Nobody was about except several little court pages who played a game of draughts in the sun. Dressed in white tunics and red ribbons, they looked charming.

"Do you know where First Avenue is?"

"It is just up the river from our house," answered Nobuko. "Do you know somebody who lives there?"

"It is late." Yoshitsune rose. "We had best be getting back before Konnomaru's beard turns white."

"He went off with grandfather early this morning. They will

just be returning, I think. So if we hurry, perhaps they will not even have missed you."

A few evenings later Konnomaru entered Yoshitsune's room carrying a dark, hooded cloak like the one he was wearing.

"Where are we going?" Yoshitsune asked eagerly. He was always ready for danger.

"I have arranged a meeting," Konnomaru replied. "The men who will take you east to your brother Yoritomo wish to see you."

In quick understanding, Yoshitsune nodded. "They want to know if they must lead me or if I am strong enough to lead them. Am I right, Konnomaru?"

Konnomaru smiled.

As they proceeded down the street, Konnomaru led the way. Both he and Yoshitsune were heavily masked, but they almost ran headlong into a group of Heike samurai as they left the gay quarters, and Konnomaru obviously worried over it.

It was the Hour of the Ox. The streets ahead of them were dark and quiet. Following one twisting alley after another, Konnomaru stopped at a house near Rashomon Gate at the southern end of Kyoto. Pushing through a gap in the wattled hedge, they crossed the broken veranda and passed through musty rooms to the back. The garden behind the ruined house was silent.

"We'll wait here," Konnomaru said.

Yoshitsune stared at the brambles and overgrown thickets. The place depressed him.

"Where are they?" His voice was impatient.

Almost as he spoke, four heavily cloaked men appeared. With their cloaks billowing behind them, they looked like the winged demons of Kurama Mountain. They seemed to have arrived from nowhere. They were Tengu indeed.

They turned to Konnomaru. Yoshitsune remained hidden in

the shadows.

"And the boy?"

The words made Yoshitsune furious. And yet he understood. He alone could make them respect him. He drew himself up to his full height and stepped forward to speak in a stiff commanding tone.

"Enough. This is no game of hide-and-seek with a child as a pawn. These intrigues are hateful, and I have no more stomach for waiting. The Genji have hidden in the mountains and crept through back alleys too long. In another month, the summer will be over. We shall leave for the east."

Astonishment was followed swiftly by deep respect on the surrounding faces. They had seen that he was not a boy but a grown man, born to lead and to command. Yoshitsune was sure that in one moment of surprise he had won not only their duty but their allegiance. He would be their leader. He stepped forward again, his anger gone, replaced by a flooding warmth. With a smile he accepted the unspoken vow of all.

"And now, if you like, I shall tell you their names," said Konnomaru wryly.

Laughter relieved the tension, and they sat down to talk.

"Tsugunobu Sato and Tadanobu Sato . . . brothers. Kijiro Yoshioka and Kisanta Yoshioka . . . also brothers."

The Heike had redoubled their vigilance. Hourly reports were brought to Kiyomori either at Rokuhara or at his mansion on West Eighth Avenue. A house-to-house search was begun.

One morning in the middle of the eighth month, a page announced the captain of the guard. The captain drew close to the raised part of the floor, where Kiyomori lay behind his curtains of state. The blinds had not yet been raised, and the room was dim. Kiyomori's voice sounded tired.

"Yes, captain."

"He seems to have vanished. Perhaps he has already left the

city." The captain said.

"Impossible. The city is surrounded by a twenty-four hour watch. Every gate is guarded and road barriers have been established along all routes."

The captain sighed. "Then he is extraordinarily well hidden. We cannot find him."

Kiyomori grew angry. "Search the houses again. Post soldiers on every avenue, every alley."

"The people resent us. They grow troubled at the sight of so many soldiers. And . . ."

"And what?"

"And the soldiers do not always behave very well. This business has stirred up the people's old grievances."

"I have done my best for them. I cannot force Goshirakawa to lessen the imperial taxes. I know they are resentful. But Yoshitsune must be found."

"I understand. I know what difficulties you have had. We will naturally continue to search."

The captain bowed his way out of the room.

"Take me to First Avenue," said Yoshitsune one night.

Nobuko shook her head. "Oh no. Please, my lord. It is too near the Imperial Palace, and there are sure to be many soldiers."

"Nevertheless, you must take me there. There is someone I have to see."

"Your mother."

Yoshitsune smiled and nodded. "You know everything, little one. Do you know the house?"

Nobuko lowered her eyes.

"We will be very careful," he reassured her. "But I must go."

It was a small but pretty house just off the Kamo River. The clever little girl found an unguarded gap in the hedge, and together they slipped in. Nobuko remained hidden in the thickets to keep watch.

In the northeastern garden there was a cool spring. A little distance off were tall-stemmed forest trees whose thick leaves made airy tunnels of shade. It was the sort of garden that would be at its best in the fall, with brier roses and large beds of chrysanthemums. The garden had a wild and lonely look about it.

Yoshitsune crept among the shadows to the house. Somewhere a shutter had broken loose, he could hear it banging in the wind. He shuddered. What a depressing place! He hurried on to the eastern side of the house, anxious to find his mother, hoping to find a way to enter unobserved. He swung himself over the low railing of an outer corridor and tried a screen. To his surprise it slid open easily. The room he entered was bare save for two or three scattered clothing boxes. Gently he slid the inner screen open and moved silently down the hall past empty, quiet rooms.

He pushed the door at the end of the hall and heard someone chanting prayers. He peered through a hole in one of the screens and almost gasped aloud. A kneeling figure in grape-colored robes was outlined by the light of altar candles. A sprig of blossoms rested at the foot of a small bronze Buddha. He remembered that it was the time of the O-Bon, the Feast of the Dead, when the living make offerings to their souls.

The fragrance of burning incense was heavy. Crouched in the hall, Yoshitsune waited, not wanting to disturb his mother's prayers. Finally, she rose and passed from the inner chapel through the hanging curtains into the back of the house. Yoshitsune followed her.

To brighten the darkness of the room, the maidservant lit a dim lamp and retired, leaving Tokiwa alone. A low writing desk and a dressing table were all the room contained. The blinds had been raised, and she sat staring out into the garden.

"Mother? *Okasan?*" His voice was hoarse from emotion and suppressed excitement.

Tokiwa's hand flew to her throat and her startled eyes turned to him.

Shock prevented her from speaking for several moments. "Ushiwaka?" she whispered. That had been his childhood name before the ceremony of initiation into manhood.

"Yes. It is Ushiwaka." He rushed forward and dropped to his knees before her. "I have come to say goodby. I could not leave without once more seeing your face."

Tokiwa had heard of her son's disappearance from the monastery and had spent her days praying for his safety. She was sad that he had not taken his vows. *Kokoro no yami,* a darkness of the heart, is the love of parents for children, she thought.

"You must understand, mother," he said urgently. "Please do understand. I am Yoshitomo's son. I cannot lead the life of a priest and leave my father unavenged."

Tokiwa shook her head sadly. "I knew this would happen. Even as a child you were restless like a small caged bird. Oh, Ushiwaka, why must there be more bloodshed. Where will it end? The Genji and the Heike, one war after another."

"Our country is in trouble," said Yoshitsune. "The arrogance of the Heike is unbearable. They leave their lands and do nothing but play at court. They overtax the people. It isn't only to avenge my father that I must lead the life of a warrior. I have had letters from Yoritomo. Even the Heike in the east are with us. Kiyomori may have brought peace for a while, but he has done nothing to change the lives of the people. If we do not act, the country will be ruined."

"Kiyomori is not a bad man. He has tried."

"How can you, of all people, speak kindly of Kiyomori?" cried Yoshitsune.

Tokiwa sighed. "He has been kind to me, in his own way," she said quietly. "And he spared the lives of my children."

Yoshitsune was too shocked to speak for a moment. "But the things he made you do to pay for it . . . and he murdered your husband," Yoshitsune finally choked out. Then he added, more calmly, "I know I am young, and that there are still many things I don't understand. You may have reasons for feeling as you do. But I am Yoshitomo's son and a warrior, and I must fight for what I believe."

Tokiwa's pale face drooped. "You must do as you think right," she said. "I am a woman, and I cannot bear to think of more bloodshed. But I understand. Only remember, if there must be war again, do not let it be a pointless one. Fight for what you think is right, but do not let arrogance and cruelty enter your heart."

Tears shone in Yoshitsune's eyes. "I shall remember. Thank you for understanding."

Tokiwa smiled sadly. "Go safely, Ushiwaka."

# Benkei at Gojo Bridge

One day early in the ninth month the first damp chill of autumn gripped the capital. Yoshitsune knew that in the mountains the leaves would be starting to turn and the chirruping of autumn insects would fill the pine forests. He scrawled a hasty note to Konnomaru, drew a rough cloak over his shoulders and a scarf over his face, and went through the gate at the back of the garden.

There was one more thing he wanted to do before he left Kyoto. He had a strange wish to see Rokuhara, Kiyomori's great estate across the Kamo River. It would amuse him to walk right under Kiyomori's nose.

He dawdled along the river's edge, toying with the iron-ribbed warrior's fan hidden in his sleeve, a present from Konnomaru. Long and heavy, it was used to signal troops in battle and would serve him also as a weapon. When folded, it had the strength of a long iron bar.

Across the Gojo Bridge, a long, tree-lined avenue led to Roku-hara. There were houses on either side for Kiyomori's family and retainers, and large stables and a falconry had been built near the river. People hurried everywhere. From a clump of bushes,

Yoshitsune watched a group of soldiers march through the two-storied gate to their barracks near the stables. Warriors arrived, their horses' hooves flying and creating clouds of dust.

Yoshitsune clenched his teeth. Someday, the Genji would have Rokuhara, he decided. He waited awhile, hoping to catch a glimpse of Kiyomori himself. But it was late in the afternoon, the Hour of the Monkey, and he had to get back.

Returning the way he had come, Yoshitsune heard a commotion. It seemed to come from the direction of Gojo Bridge. He paused for a moment, considering whether he had best cross the river farther downstream to avoid the crowd. But curiosity, as always, overcame his common sense, and he continued toward the bridge.

A large crowd had gathered at both ends of the wide wooden bridge. Their shouts and cries mingled with the thundering of pounding feet on the bridge itself. Arranging his scarf to cover all but his eyes, Yoshitsune pushed his way to the edge of the bridge. At his feet sprawled an elegantly dressed samurai, panting and trying to get up. Yoshitsune laughed and helped him. The samurai gave him a terrified glance and darted past Yoshitsune into the crowd.

A great bellowing roar of laughter rang in the air. Yoshitsune peered through the late afternoon gloom. At the far end of the bridge, the most gigantic figure Yoshitsune had ever seen loomed toward him. The sleeves of his monk's robes were tied back, and the huge muscular arms gleamed with perspiration. The features of the face beneath the powerful, shaven head were strong, but the eyes shone with humor, and laughter came from the wide mouth. In the man's fist was a sword—but with the scabbard still on, it was only a blunt weapon.

Benkei! That's who this giant was! The powerful *yamabushi* had come down from Mount Hiei to the capital for money to erect a new temple. He had not been able to persuade the imperial treasury to give him the money, so he had taken matters into his own hands. He stood at Gojo Bridge several afternoons a week. He never hurt the common people, but whenever a samurai or a court noble passed across the bridge, he knocked him down with the flat of his sheathed sword and took the gentleman's money.

Those who had been attacked had appealed for justice. But Goshirakawa and Kiyomori did not want to anger the powerful monks on Mount Hiei; and since Benkei had murdered no one, he had simply been ignored. It was hoped that one day he would meet his match, or simply have had enough and go away.

Yoshitsune, as he stood there watching the enormous warrior monk swinging his arms, felt more sympathy than anger toward him. The whole thing struck him as funny. Wouldn't it be a marvelous joke if he solved Kiyomori's problem for him? Granted, Yoshitsune was half the giant's size. Granted, he ought not to get mixed up in a public commotion. Kiyomori's soldiers might be anywhere. But the thing was too tempting. He couldn't resist. He was determined to vanquish Benkei.

"Ho there!"

The ringing challenge reached Benkei's ears.

Benkei's shrewd eyes peered across the bridge. When he spied the graceful figure coming toward him he threw back his head and howled with laughter.

"You young puppy. Are you challenging me?"

Yoshitsune laughed with equal humor. "I am."

"But I have no quarrel with you."

"I shall begin one, then."

"You should be spanked, not battled with." Benkei could hardly talk for laughing.

"You think so?" said Yoshitsune softly. His eyes narrowed.

Benkei continued to mock him. Anger rose like a brittle flame in Yoshitsune's throat, but he knew better than to let anger cloud his judgment in combat. The monks and the mountain Tengu had taught him well. He breathed deeply to cool his brain.

From the folds of his sleeve he drew the iron-ribbed fan, holding it lightly but firmly in his strong grasp. He threw off his cloak, wrapping it round his forearm carefully.

The *yamabushi* stopped laughing. Obviously, Yoshitsune decided, the man had realized that the challenge was serious. Yoshitsune was delighted. His muscles felt like coiled steel, eager for the chance to jump out. He moved forward.

The two circled each other on the narrow bridge. The crowd was hushed and wary. This was no laughing matter at all, no mock battle with a pompous courtier.

Yoshitsune moved with litheness and grace. The energy of his body, the control he held over it, delighted him. And with almost equal delight he watched Benkei's face. He could see the thoughts in the mind of the monk, the wonder and the questions: Who was this masked young man? It was clear he had been trained well. But how? Who was he? Not a warrior, in that white silk tunic, unarmed and barefoot. Not a priest, with his full head of hair in its simple knot. A commoner? Not with that grace and boldness.

A swift stab of pain put an end to Benkei's thoughts. With the agility of a monkey Yoshitsune leaped under Benkei's guard and swung the iron-ribbed fan. Only a quick reflex saved Benkei from being completely winded, and the blow landed on his side instead of directly in his diaphragm. But the blow was hard as it jabbed his ribs. Surprised at Yoshitsune's skill and power, Benkei stood stupefied for a split second before he jumped back.

Benkei would know better than to let his guard down again, Yoshitsune thought. Benkei raised his sheathed sword and directed a blow to the side of Yoshitsune's neck, one intended to immediately knock him out. Yoshitsune waited until the weapon was within a few inches of his head before he ducked. As he had anticipated, the weight Benkei had thrown into the movement of his arm carried him forward. Benkei barely saved himself from falling. Wheeling about, the great *yamabushi* grunted.

"Well, well. This must be stopped quickly."

"Try then," Yoshitsune invited.

They circled each other again. In a flash, Yoshitsune jabbed at Benkei's stomach with his fan. Benkei threw him off balance with his sword and landed a blow which caught Yoshitsune on the shoulder. When Benkei again raised his weapon, Yoshitsune swung his cloak in such a way that it tangled in Benkei's feet. The powerful giant lunged forward, but before he fell he landed a heavy blow on the side of Yoshitsune's head. Benkei hit the wooden planks of the bridge, which trembled with his weight. And Yoshitsune, reeling from the blow, staggered back against the railing.

They fought for nearly half an hour, neither badly injured. They were well matched, and it seemed to be a question of who tired first.

The crowd was amazed. The *yamabushi* was one of the most feared warriors in Kyoto, and a young man, unknown to anyone, was keeping him at bay for such a length of time.

When it seemed as though with one final swing Benkei would crush Yoshitsune with his very force, Yoshitsune gathered every ounce of his failing strength. Benkei came rushing headlong, the sword raised, still in its scabbard. In a split second Yoshitsune leaped sideways, and, with all the force he could muster, slammed the iron-ribbed fan flat against the side of the giant's neck. For a moment, Benkei reeled, stunned. Then slowly he slumped to his knees, his head lowered.

Yoshitsune stood over him. The crowd roared.

Benkei held up his sword. He was panting heavily, and his face was ashen. Dimly, Yoshitsune heard him speak.

"Before you kill me," he said, "tell me your name. Who are you?"

Yoshitsune stared down at the kneeling figure. Gently, he pushed the sword back into Benkei's hands. "You could have unsheathed your sword at any moment," he said loudly enough for all to hear. "You have fought honorably, and I shall repay fairness for fairness. You chose not to take my life. I choose not to take yours."

"You beat me fairly."

"You fought with honor."

As Yoshitsune bent his head to return the fan to his sleeve, the scarf finally slipped from his face. Benkei had seen such a face before, once, from a distance. The features were mature now, no longer those of the child he had glimpsed years ago on Kurama Mountain; but there could be no mistake.

Yoshitsune glanced at him sharply, sensing immediately that Benkei had recognized him. For a moment he held his breath. One cry from the warrior priest and his freedom, probably his life, was at an end.

Benkei rose and bowed deeply. The massive face was somber when he spoke at last. "With your permission," he said in a low voice, "you are such a master as I would serve, Yoshitsune of the Genji." He waited silently, bowing still, for the reply.

Konnomaru stood on the western bank of the river. His face was stern, and there was pain in his heart as he watched. Darkness fell on the river before two figures appeared suddenly at his side.

"Konnomaru! Have you been here all the time?"

"I fear for you, Yoshitsune." The old man shook his head. "You court death too bravely. You must leave Kyoto immediately now. Any one of those in the crowd might have recognized you."

Yoshitsune was suddenly sorry, not for himself, but for Konnomaru.

"I promise I shall not run from you again until we reach the east," he said gravely.

"I shall not be going with you," sighed Konnomaru. "I must stay here for a while. But I fear none of your escort is a match for you. Danger seeks you out. What is to become of you?"

A deep voice said quietly, "I shall not leave his side."

The towering form loomed behind Yoshitsune. "No harm shall come to him while I live."

"Never fear, Konnomaru. Benkei will curb me," said Yoshitsune, laughing mischievously.

Konnomaru shook his head, slowly and doubtfully.

"Konnomaru is right, master," said Benkei. "You cannot remain in Kyoto. We must leave tonight."

"But we need provisions."

Benkei smiled. "Leave such things to me, my lord."

"You must admit, Konnomaru," said Yoshitsune, "for a change I did myself an excellent service in courting danger. I have gained in a single thrust a friend and a one-man bodyguard."

Benkei beamed.

Then quickly they made their plans.

# Uji

A group of begging monks in tattered cassocks, their heads shaven, lowered themselves onto the steps of Rashomon Gate. Rattling their prayer chains, a begging bowl on each knee, they began to chant the *nembutsu,* the prayer for salvation.

"*Namu Amida butsu. Namu Amida butsu.*"

Adoration to the Buddha of boundless light and life.

And they fingered the one hundred eight beads of their prayer chains, each bead representing one of the worldly cares of man.

The chanting attracted the attention of the captain of the guard on duty at the gate.

"I recognize that prayer," the captain said to his companion. "Last week I attended the minister of the left on the imperial pilgrimage to Mount Hiei. A priest named Honen has formed a new sect based on salvation by faith alone."

The other was amused. "Just faith? No offerings and rituals?"

"Yes. All one has to do is call on the name of the Amida Buddha. As those monks are doing over there. That is the way to attain true enlightenment and be one with the Lord of the Universe."

"I am curious. Let us talk to them a little."

The two strolled to where the monks clustered on the steps near the great pillar. They found enlightenment, but not of the sort they had expected. The largest of the group, a giant when he straightened up, felled the captain with a single blow. Another attacked his companion. Bowls and prayer chains flew to the ground; and a moment later, the monks escaped through the Rashomon Gate, cassocks flapping in the wind.

In the dense woods to the south of the capital, the monks were awaited. The light of a crescent moon filtered through the rising mist as they made their way through the wild, autumn grasslands toward the woods.

A fierce exultation swept through Yoshitsune as he raced through the tall grass. His ears were sharpened to the cry of the birds and to the hushed calls of his companions. Reaching the edge of the woods, he plunged into the thicket, leaping as lightly over the trailing vines as a wild deer. His hooded cloak was soon drenched with dew, and he removed it to move about more easily. He alone had worn a hood to hide his warrior's knot. They had refused to cut his hair, and he was glad. He had had enough of looking like a monk.

The sound of pawing hooves filtered through the trees. To his left he could hear the rustling movements of his companions. They were probably searching for him. Yoshitsune had long been adept at moving soundlessly. In another moment he had broken through the dense brush and now stood at the edge of a small clearing. Several horses were tethered to a sturdy tree, strong fast horses from the eastern plains of Japan.

Except for the horses, the clearing was empty. The animals were restless and jostled each other. Suddenly, one of the horses tossed his head and, rearing onto his hind legs, broke loose. He galloped twice across the clearing, his fury mounting as he saw no escape. As the horse paused to regain his wind, Yoshitsune stepped forward and came straight toward him, holding out his hand and staring into the animal's eyes. His voice was low and easy as he approached. The horse was still until Yoshitsune was only a foot away. Then he reared back, his forelegs pawing at the air, missing Yoshitsune by inches. Faster than the eye could watch, Yoshitsune sunk his fist into the thick mane and swung himself onto the horse's back. The battle lasted fifteen minutes. The young man won; the horse stood quietly, accepting his master.

"Well done."

"You have the skill of the great eastern horsemen."

At the edge of the clearing stood a band of monks, smiling and applauding the excellent horsemanship of their young chieftain.

"Come, we must hurry now. We are expected."

Yoshitsune looked with pride at his band. Small though they were in number, each was a fine warrior, powerful, skilled, and alert. And their loyalty to the clan of the Genji and to himself was unquestionable. Give me always such men, thought Yoshitsune, and we cannot fail. The Sato brothers, Tsugunobu and Tadanobu, who looked so much alike, were serious, careful, deeply devoted to the cause of the Genji. Kisanta and Kijiro Yoshioka, whose wit and gaiety would enliven the long journey ahead, resembled each other not at all. Yet their brotherhood was obvious in their concern for each other, and they were equally expert with the bow and arrow and with the ladies. And Benkei. His great love for Yoshitsune and his tremendous resourcefulness had already proved invaluable. The band was also accompanied by trustworthy retainers.

The five warriors mounted their horses. Their retainers would follow on foot until more horses could be found.

Kisanta laughed. "We must be quite a sight."

They did indeed look odd. Their begging robes did not exactly match their expert horsemanship.

"By your leave, my lord," said Benkei. "I have made arrangements with an old friend for your reception at Uji."

"Uji? But that is eleven miles south of the capital. Surely it would be faster to head directly east."

"Faster, but less safe. By now Kiyomori will have sent troops after us toward the east." Benkei scowled. "I wish I had not had to kill the captain of the guard. But there was no choice. No one is permitted to leave the city after dark without imperial permission. It won't have taken Kiyomori long to guess the reason for the captain's death."

Yoshitsune nodded. Benkei was right.

"Our friend at Uji will give us supplies. He insisted that your visit would give him pleasure."

"Your friend is most kind." Yoshitsune paused. "And his sympathies?"

Benkei grinned. "He is a most trusted and devoted follower of your brother Yoritomo. No one at the capital suspects this yet, and he serves a very useful purpose spying at the court of ex-Emperor Goshirakawa. He is, in fact, a counselor of the fourth rank."

"His name?" Yoshitsune asked.

"Shigeyori Taro Kawagoe."

Benkei led the way along a narrow path that passed through the woods to the edge of the Kamo River.

"It is best to cross here, where it is narrow. Farther south, the crossing is more difficult."

Men and horses plunged into the river. They rode south until gradually they emerged from the wild countryside into cultivated fields of wheat and rice. The roar of the nearby Uji River as it beat against fish-weirs was deafening. Icy blasts stung their faces, and the winds scattered a storm of leaves. Heavy wreaths of autumn mist swathed the moon and trailed across the sky.

The nightwatchman saw them approaching Shigeyori's estate and ran to greet them. He led them through the gate, and after they dismounted he hurried the horses off to the stables. A servant escorted them to a room in the eastern wing, where a charcoal brazier and dry clothes awaited them all. After the men changed into the informal country dress provided by their host, fish and steaming bowls of rice were brought with a large jug of sake.

The servant bowed. "My master sends his most humble apologies that he is not here to greet you. He has just sent his groom to announce that he will arrive shortly. You are please to consider his house as your own."

While the others passed the jug of wine around Yoshitsune wandered out to the garden. The sound of a lute and a sweet voice humming floated to him on the night air. It seemed to come from the western wing, and he crept around the corner of the house. In a dim room sat a girl, surrounded by her attendants. In spite of the late hour, and the rudeness of invading a lady's privacy, Yoshitsune had a lonely desire to see her. He entered the room, speaking softly and quickly.

"Don't be afraid. I won't hurt you. Your music drew me to this room, and I felt I could not leave without at least having spoken to you. Please do not cry out." The girl gasped and crept back behind her curtains. But for some reason she did not cry out.

"Don't hide from me, I beg you," said Yoshitsune. His one glimpse of the small, slender figure and lovely face had enchanted him. "At least tell me your name."

Silence. And then, in a small voice, "Kyo-no-Kimi. I am Shigeyori's daughter. Please go away."

Suddenly ashamed of himself, Yoshitsune murmured an apology and left the room. That night he hardly slept. His host Shigeyori's daughter! He could not get her out of his mind. In the morning he crept again to the western wing.

A tall screen hid the room from view, but he could hear scraps of conversation.

"Come, my lady, you have eaten nothing. Try just a little of the fish and wine. You must keep up your strength. What will the empress say if we bring you back to her pale and unwell?"

Unable to contain himself any longer, Yoshitsune burst into the room, to the great confusion of the women. There was much fluttering of fans and an attempt to screen Kyo-no-Kimi from view.

"Do not be alarmed. You must know who I am," said Yoshitsune.

"Really," flustered an elderly gentlewoman. "This is not at all the sort of thing my lady is accustomed to. As lady-in-waiting to the empress she does not encounter such rudeness." Yoshitsune ignored the remark, although it gave him a start.

A sudden gust of wind knocked down the screen in front of Kyo-no-Kimi. In her distress she appeared to Yoshitsune the most exquisite creature he had ever seen. She was dressed elaborately in scarlet embroidered court robes over several underkimonos. The edges peeped out at her neck, one under the other, deep

lavender, pale green, and white. Her long hair framed the pale
oval of her face and fell gently onto her shoulders.

Yoshitsune looked straight into her eyes and smiled. And
though she still seemed frightened, Kyo-no-Kimi smiled back, a
small, wondering smile that made Yoshitsune's heart pound.

"He is certainly handsome," said one of the ladies.

"But don't you know who he is?" replied another. "It would be
terribly dangerous for our mistress if anything were to happen
between them."

"Do you think it could?"

"You have eyes in your head," came the severe reply. "You
have only to look at them to see what is happening."

Yoshitsune still stood before Kyo-no-Kimi, letting the bright-
ness of his new feeling flood him. He felt for a moment as though
he held some shining crystal thing in his hands, something which
the slightest motion would shatter into a thousand pieces. He
had never seen such marvelous beauty, and he vowed then that
one day she would belong to him alone.

Still she had not yet spoken to him.

"Please say something," he begged. "I want to hear your voice.
Shall you tell your father I was here?"

"No," she whispered. "He would be angry. I am already
betrothed."

Yoshitsune's face darkened. "When are you to be married?"

"Not for a long time. I am lady-in-waiting to her highness the
empress, and she does not wish me to leave her."

Yoshitsune smiled. "Then do not count on it. I shall be back
before then."

There was a stir among the ladies. But Kyo-no-Kimi, Yoshitsune noted, continued to smile.

In the distance there was noise of laughter and footsteps.
Others were coming. Yoshitsune dared stay no longer. On the
floor near the edge of her robe rested a beautiful fan of hinoki
wood hung with silken tassels. Yoshitsune picked it up and hid

it quickly in his sleeve. Kyo-no-Kimi pretended not to notice, but Yoshitsune knew she had. They gazed at each other in silence for a moment. Then, with a last lingering look, he slipped out as quickly as he had come.

"You are welcome to my home," said Shigeyori as Yoshitsune entered the central room where the men were gathered. "If there is anything you wish, you have only to mention it. I was just saying to Benkei how good it is to see him again. I understand he no longer occupies Gojo Bridge."

Benkei grinned. "I feel certain I shall not be missed."

Shigeyori grew serious then. "My groom has just brought a message from the capital. It seems a bamboo-cutter saw all that happened at the Rashomon Gate and reported it. Kiyomori's soldiers are searching in all directions. It would not be wise for you to remain here much longer. I have arranged for everything. Three packhorses carry enough supplies to last for several weeks, and there are ample horses for your retainers."

"I can only thank you in words now," said Yoshitsune. "In time, you shall be well rewarded for all you have done."

"Your successful journey will be reward enough," said Shigeyori. "One thing more. I have been able to find these. I think you may find them useful."

He clapped his hands and three retainers dragged in several large clothing boxes. Shigeyori opened them. The treasure within brought a smile even to the faces of the serious Sato brothers, while Kijiro and Kisanta whooped with glee. Shigeyori smiled at their pleasure and presented the contents. From the first box he took out several suits of armor. Bowing deeply, he presented the most elaborate to Yoshitsune. The breastplate, shoulder pieces, and quartered skirt were of metal lacquered with silver. To show his rank, the lacings were of purple silk braid. The leg and forearm protectors were of padded scarlet brocade. The metal helmet, with its wide neck protector, was adorned with gilded horns. The underrobe and trousers were of scarlet silk. It was indeed a most splendid suit of armor.

The armor of the Sato brothers was lacquered black and laced with crimson. For the Yoshioka brothers, black laced with blue. And for Benkei, black laced with white. There was also a suit for each of the retainers, rawhide plate laced with leather thongs. Their metal helmets were painted with the Genji *mon*, the clan crest worn by common soldiers.

But the most prized gift of all was the sword that Shigeyori gave to each, the curved Japanese sword, the *nihon-to*, which is the soul of the samurai, to be wielded only in honorable battle for a worthy cause. It was accompanied by the short sword. Only a samurai, a warrior, was permitted to carry both. And in the hilt of the long sword was tucked a small dagger, its use—honorable suicide rather than capture by the enemy.

In the third chest were bows and quivers of arrows for all, the "twenty-five arrow" quiver, the last arrow of which was never used since it was intended to safeguard its owner after death. Kijiro and Kisanta, whose prowess with the bow and arrow was unsurpassed, tried the bows and marveled at their suppleness and strength.

By the time all was ready it was the Hour of the Cock and darkness had fallen. The men sat in the unlit room and silently passed a jug of sake from one to the other in a farewell drink. Each seemed to be thinking of the long and dangerous journey ahead and the importance of getting Yoshitsune safely to the east.

Finally Yoshitsune rose. With a deep and respectful bow, Shigeyori led them from the room. The horses were ready, and the small band mounted. They paused in a silent farewell and then quickly rode off into the heavy autumn mist.

# Journey to the East

They rode north again, into the Eastern Hills. The dense fog formed a shield, and dark outer cloaks hid the gleam of their armor. Tsugunobu and Tadanobu rode on ahead, while Kijiro and Kisanta remained in the rear. Benkei rode by Yoshitsune's side. From time to time, he glanced at Yoshitsune.

"If you do not wish me to know, I shall not ask again," said Benkei softly. "But if there is something wrong, and it is within my power to help, you know you have only to say so."

Although Yoshitsune's thoughts were far away, he rode easily on the wild, restless horse, handling him perfectly. The concern in Benkei's voice touched him. He had never completely trusted anyone before. But he knew suddenly he could trust Benkei.

"Shigeyori has a daughter," said Yoshitsune. "Did you know that?"

Benkei nodded.

"She was at Uji," said Yoshitsune softly.

Benkei looked surprised, and Yoshitsune understood. Shigeyori had said nothing of his daughter's presence at Uji—obviously on purpose. As devoted as he was to the Genji, Shigeyori would not want his daughter involved with a penniless outlaw. He had

obviously gone to too much trouble to make Kyo-no-Kimi's position safe at court. No matter which way the political winds blew,
she would be safe with the empress.

"She is so beautiful, Benkei. And I—I was very rude. I broke
into her private apartments. I know it was wrong of me. I could
not help it."

"It will be as you want it to be," said Benkei softly, the tender-
ness in his voice belying his ferocious appearance.

Yoshitsune's thoughts brightened a little. It seemed so impossible, that Kyo-no-Kimi should be his. And yet, it must be so.
No one else would ever do, now that he had seen her.

Just then, Tadanobu rode back toward them.

"If we hurry, we might reach Shirakawa Pass by daybreak.
Once through the pass, we shall be much safer."

Tadanobu wheeled his horse sharply, and the three plunged
down into a narrow valley and up the steep slope to the next
ridge, where Tsugunobu waited. The lower Eastern Hills, now
beneath them, were cloudy with mist. Before them, the mountains rose darkly, and they could hear the thunder of a waterfall
close by. They waited for Kisanta and Kijiro before continuing
on to the next ridge, quiet, listening.

An unexpected sound disturbed them, and they were instantly
alert, listening sharply. There was no mistake. Hoarse cries and
shouts and the hoofbeats of horses, pounding heavily with their
weight of fully armored men.

Heike soldiers! And there could be no doubt of their mission.
The Heike were coming from the east.

"Go back! Go back into the trees," said Tsugunobu.

When Yoshitsune did not move, Tsugunobu's voice grew
urgent. "Please, my lord. If they catch sight of us, it will be a
bloody encounter."

Anger darkened Yoshitsune's face. "I am not afraid of a hand-
ful of Heike soldiers. Let them come and learn what the Genji
warriors can do."

Tadanobu leaned close to Benkei and whispered, "He is fearless. But you must persuade him to retreat to safety."

Benkei cleared his throat and spoke cautiously, "Even if we win in battle, my lord, should one escape and return to court to give away our position, it would endanger our whole purpose. We should arrive in the east to find a whole army to deal with before we are ready. So far, all Kiyomori knows is that a few outlawed Genji have helped you to escape. He does not yet know that we are riding to Yoritomo. Please, my lord, reconsider. There is a cave I know less than five hundred yards away."

Yoshitsune paused, still trying to overcome his desire to fight his enemies and listen to what he knew was sound reasoning.

Tadanobu added calmly, "It is necessary, above all else, that you reach the east in safety. We cannot triumph unless you remain alive, my lord."

Yoshitsune said nothing, only stared ahead. And the Heike saw him. He raised his arm and pointed silently to the high ridge above.

"It is too late," cried Kijiro. "They have seen us. They will be upon us in a few minutes."

On the crest of the ridge, outlined against the sky, some two dozen armored warriors gestured excitedly and reined in their horses. Shouting, they rode furiously down toward the valley.

"There aren't many," said Benkei. "And though the Heike are good with bows when they shoot from the ground, their horsemanship isn't as good as ours, and it throws their aim off." He turned to Yoshitsune. "If you go back into the trees and keep out of sight, they will take us for a band of thieves. It will make them think they can overcome us easily, and we can scatter them more quickly."

Again the suggestion made sense, and unwillingly Yoshitsune turned his horse and moved in behind the trees. It bothered him to have to just watch. But he had no choice.

Quickly the men donned their helmets and ranged themselves

in a line, drawing their bows taut.

Yoshitsune watched as Kisanta drew an arrow from his quiver and, locking his fingers around the heavy rattan bow, arched it and waited. In another second, the first of the Heike soldiers emerged into the valley, riding as swiftly as the wind rides across the valley floor. Kisanta aimed his shaft, drew in his breath, and let the arrow fly. It drove cleanly through the first rider's neck-plate, and he fell headlong to the ground. Within a split second, Kijiro's arrow skewered the throat of the second rider. A battery of arrows from both sides skimmed through the air, and the riders came together in a rush. Drawn swords flashed and glittered in hand-to-hand combat to the death.

From his hiding place, Yoshitsune kept track of his men. His sweeping glance found the Sato brothers.

He saw Tadanobu thrust his sword into the neck of one Heike warrior, and there was an ugly, strangling sound as the man fell. But Tadanobu's back was unguarded, and though he turned swiftly to avoid a death blow, his opponent's sword fell with enough force to knock him from his horse. Crashing steel and the screams of horses filled the air. Swords pierced armored sleeves, helmets, leg guards, and blood and dust mingled on the ground.

Tsugunobu, seeing four horsemen plunge at his brother, rushed to attack. Benkei, having felled two with the mighty strength of his sword, plunged after Tsugunobu.

Several feet away, Kisanta and Kijiro struggled in close conflict with three times their number. Just beyond, Heike and Genji retainers, most of whom were already dismounted, grappled on foot, hacking at arms and legs until six or seven men sprawled on their faces, wounded or dead.

Having felled his immediate opponent, Benkei looked around. The Genji fought valiantly, but they were still greatly outnumbered. There was no time to think. Three Heike soldiers rode fast upon him, their horses' tails streaming in the wind. A loud voice challenged him.

"You wear Genji armor. Who are you? Thieves, I imagine, with stolen spoils." The speaker laughed harshly. "I shall rip such cursed armor from your back."

"With your two retainers, you are bold indeed to attack me," called Benkei. "Come on, all three of you."

And he wheeled his horse and drew forth an arrow. The four horses crossed and recrossed each other's paths as Benkei whirled away, each time trying to retain enough distance to let go an arrow. Benkei's horsemanship was a brilliant spectacle. Whirling, dodging, feinting, the combatants rode furiously. Benkei shot an arrow. It reached its mark, and one of his opponents fell. He drew his sword and sped in for a close attack on the second. But the one who had called out in challenge beat him off. For nearly fifteen minutes, Benkei fought them both. Then a third and a fourth joined in against him. Even Benkei's powerful strength was beginning to give way. The others, meantime, had all they could do to manage their part of the battle.

It was too much for Yoshitsune. He pressed forward and in a hoarse voice he lashed out, "You will deal with me."

Sword raised, a surge of furious anger flooding his eyes, Yoshitsune rode into the middle of the Heike soldiers, slashing right and left. His proud carriage on the wild stallion, as well as his deadly sword arm, caused the Heike to fall back, as if they were dealing with more than an ordinary man. He fought like a demon riding on a whirlwind, and when the Hour of the Tiger drew to a close, at sunrise, the battle ended.

Among the dead were two Genji retainers and most of the Heike soldiers, their red banners scattered in the dust. In the pale light of dawn, the Genji sat on the ground and rested, exhausted.

"Three of them managed to escape," brooded Tadanobu.

"We owe you our lives." Benkei smiled wryly at Yoshitsune. "Had you not ridden out when you did, I'm afraid we should have fared badly."

Kijiro's laughter echoed through the valley. "And we, the best of the Genji warriors."

They looked at Yoshitsune with loyalty and admiration. He had sacrificed his own safety for theirs. His courage had saved them from certain death.

Moved by the devotion of such powerful men, tears sprang to Yoshitsune's eyes. He shook his head. "On the contrary," he said. "It was you who saved mine. I came in only at the end."

The men made no answer. But Yoshitsune sensed that their lives were his to command forever, that the strong bond that had grown between them that morning would never be broken.

"I am worried about the three who escaped," said Tadanobu. "They would have to be stupid indeed not to have guessed who we are. In another hour, the news will have reached Kiyomori. And then not one tree in these hills will offer a safe hiding place."

"And we dare not travel by day. It is light already, and it won't be long before another group of soldiers spots us." Kisanta gripped his left arm ruefully. "I don't think we are up to another such battle."

Kijiro noticed his brother's arm and rushed to his side in concern. Blood trickled from a long gash on his forearm. "Really," he said, "you need not wait forever to mention the fact that you are wounded." He tore a strip from the edge of his undertunic and bound up his brother's arm.

"The wound should be cleaned properly," said Benkei.

Tsugunobu stood up. "I have a friend who lives near here," he said, "just on the other side of that ridge." He pointed to the northeast. "He will help us."

"Can he be trusted?" Yoshitsune asked.

"He is a man of peace, a priest. His home is here in the Eastern Hills." There was a wistfulness in Tsugunobu's voice, and Yoshitsune wondered if so great a warrior could have a longing for just such a life.

"But won't he inform some powerful temple about us?" persisted Kijiro.

Tsugunobu shook his head. "He has no patience either with warring temples or warring clans. He is a great poet and lives in meditation. He roams all over the land. He has even been to the east and knows Tokimasa of the Hojo, your brother's father-in-law, quite well," he said, looking at Yoshitsune.

"Then let us go to him," answered Yoshitsune. "I think I know who this friend of yours is. His Buddhist name is Saigyo, isn't it?"

Tsugunobu smiled and nodded, surprised.

"I used to hear of him at the Kurama monastery," said Yoshitsune. "He was not very popular with the Abbot—or with the court. He was once yoshikiyo of the imperial guards with a promising career before him, until he suddenly disappeared to wander these hills. I understand he is a man of great understanding and knowledge."

The band mounted as they spoke, and they followed Tsugunobu quickly down the other side of the slope.

# Red Leaves

It was the tenth day of the tenth month, the godless month. At the imperial court there was much excitement; everyone was preparing for one of the five great annual festivals, the Festival of Red Leaves. The dancing masters trained fine performers in the steps of the Dance of the Blue Waves and the Autumn Wind. The masters of ceremonies rehearsed the court musicians. The imperial gardens were at their best, with great swirls of red maple leaves mingling among the chrysanthemums. The royal princes and all the court noblemen were to be in attendance. The festival promised to be a more magnificent sight than it had ever been.

Before the festival, the boy-Emperor Takakura was to hold his morning audience in the presence chamber in the hall of state. Kiyomori and the ex-Emperor Goshirakawa arrived early, and retired to the small hall of ease behind the throne room for a private talk.

In spite of many differences, Goshirakawa and Kiyomori were bonded together in the face of a common enemy, the clan of the Genji. The Genji had political ideas of reform that neither Goshirakawa nor Kiyomori wished to see accomplished. They had different reasons, of course. Goshirakawa was interested only in

56

income and power for the Fujiwara clan. Kiyomori simply wanted peace for his country.

They began to discuss the problem that occupied both their minds.

"It seems incredible that Yoshitsune should slip through our grasp," commented the ex-emperor. "But even if he does escape through the Eastern Hills, where can he go?"

"He will probably try to reach Yoritomo," said Kiyomori.

"In that case, we need not worry. Tokimasa will take him in hand. The two brothers will be in captivity together instead of separately, that's all," said Goshirakawa.

"For once, my dear friend," said Kiyomori, "I think you are wrong. With the two together, there is more likely to be trouble. The Genji are few in number, but as a clan they have lost face. They will make every attempt to regain their honor."

"What can so few Genji accomplish against us? That tattered band would hardly dare attack the capital. And yet," mused Goshirakawa, "I also am uneasy about it. Has there been any news?"

"So far they have disappeared without a trace. But I have sent out soldiers, and I hope for some sort of news today or tomorrow."

A page announced that the morning audience had begun, and the two men went to the enormous imperial presence hall. There in the center of the great draperied imperial dais, sat the small figure of the thirteen-year-old emperor.

"He looks pale this morning," Kiyomori thought. He wondered if his daughter, whom he had given to Takakura as reigning empress to further unite the Heike and Fujiwara clans, were happy with this pale, young emperor. He was not strong, politically he was a pawn, yet as Japan's greatest religious symbol he was safe enough.

Before the emperor, hundreds of courtiers headed by the ministers of the left and right, the grand counselors, senior advisors and chamberlains, heads of the imperial treasury, and the members of the first through fifth ranks, the highest in the land, knelt in obeisance. All were dressed in elaborate court robes, with long trailing trousers worn to prevent fighting, and black court hats. .

Because of the festival, the morning audience was short. After a few disputes were settled, the entire court moved to the nearby Shishin Palace where festivals and ceremonies were held.

The courtiers settled themselves according to rank on the verandas and along the corridors overlooking the large courtyard where the entertainment took place. The lavish banquet, the music, and the dancing lasted far into the night.

It was eight o'clock the following morning, the Hour of the Dragon, when Kiyomori and Goshirakawa accompanied the exhausted emperor back to his imperial rooms in the Pure and Fresh Palace. As they crossed the open bridge between the palaces, a page came running up to Kiyomori and told him he was wanted at Rokuhara on an urgent matter. Hurrying immediately to his waiting carriage, Kiyomori left court.

As he rode up the tree-lined avenue to Rokuhara, he noticed that an unusually large number of soldiers both on foot and on horseback were milling excitedly about the grounds. A group of retainers rushed from the house to escort him inside. In a side chamber to the east of the central hall lay a soldier on a pile of cushions, under the care of three doctors. Two other soldiers in a state of collapse were being tended on the other side of the room. All three were covered with dirt and gaunt with fatigue. The most severely wounded was a captain of the Rokuhara Guard. As Kiyomori entered the room, the captain turned his head. Kiyomori went quickly to his side.

"Are you able to talk?"

The doctors made no comment, but it was clear from the expressions on their faces that if there was any talking to be done, it had better not wait. They moved respectfully a little to one

side and placed a cushion near the captain's head for Kiyomori
to sit upon.

Medicine had somewhat eased the captain's pain, but he could
barely speak. Kiyomori bent close to his mouth to hear his words.

"The Hour of the Tiger . . . a band of men . . . thought at
first . . . outlaws, robbers . . . too dark to see faces." The captain
paused for breath.

"What made you change your mind?"

"Well trained . . . handled arms like warriors . . . fought honorably . . . not like underhanded thieves. And then . . ."

"Yes?" urged Kiyomori.

"We were many more than they . . . all but had them beaten
back. From the trees beyond, one rode out unlike the others."
The captain's face showed his shame, but he managed to say
what he had to say. "A match for ten warriors . . . strength and
skill of a mountain demon . . . he was everywhere at once . . .
where he lifted his sword, he commanded a life. And his
men . . . when he came, they gained new strength. They had
only to feel his presence . . . and they were strong and brave
again." Three more words and the captain's voice was stilled
forever. "No ordinary man."

Whether the captain really knew whom he had fought in the
dim hours of early dawn, Kiyomori did not learn. The other two
soldiers who had escaped had no idea. Common soldiers, they had
merely followed their captain. Kiyomori, however, doubted not
at all that this extraordinary band was led by none other than
Yoshitsune of the Genji. And it was not so much the escape again
of the young Genji that disturbed him. It was rather the hidden
power, the unsuspected greatness of character that had made
such an impression on the dying captain that worried Kiyomori.
It was clear that Yoshitsune was no longer just a restless, rebel-
lious boy, but a man capable of leading and inspiring other men
and already a great warrior. It was also clear that he was attended by a group of loyal and courageous followers.

Yoshitsune opened his eyes and felt the morning surge through him. From the rough straw mat on which he lay he could look through the open window that had been cut from the bamboo wall. The mist floated in strange and lovely forms, moving like a ghost among the nearby pines. Beyond the brushwood hedge a stony path wound upward to higher ground. In the distance he could hear a low voice chanting the Four Meditations of the Law Flower. The scent of a hidden incense burner stole through the room and filled the air with a delicious fragrance.

Beneath the window was a rough-hewn desk on which brushes, inkstone, and paper lay scattered about. Someone had been copying ancient masterpieces, both Japanese and Chinese, to practice an already beautiful handwriting. On a scrap of pale blue Michinoku paper was a poem of the autumn. It was signed: Saigyo. On the Buddha shelf stood an image of Fudo, the Bodhisattva of wisdom, one of the many forms of Buddha himself. And in the far corner of the room was a folding koto. Yoshitsune had a sudden longing to hear the instrument played and to meet the great monk poet of the Eastern Hills.

Yoshitsune had been in the monastery long enough to have learned to be conscious of his own thoughts. Had he spent those years at court, he might not have learned such a discipline. Now his thoughts were of bringing honor to the name of Genji, of proving himself a great warrior, of helping reform the Japan he loved. Remembering the battle fought the day before, he was filled with a quiet pride that he had begun his warrior's life by proving himself capable in combat. He knew that he had a great deal to learn, but he also knew that his men fully acknowledged him as their leader.

He thought also of Kyo-no-Kimi.

He dressed quickly, stepped from the room onto the bamboo porch of the hut, and looked about for the other men. A little way off, on the northern side, he saw a thatched roof supported by poles of bamboo, a sort of pavilion, whose wooden floor jutted out over a mountain stream.

In the pavilion, the others were just finishing the morning meal and rose to greet their chieftain. They brought him wild fruits and steaming rice. All of them were moved by the strange beauty of the place, and they sat in silence as they sipped cup after cup of fresh green tea.

They did not mention the battle of the previous morning. It had become an unspoken bond between them, an acknowledgment of their identity and purpose, and they felt no need to discuss it. Each sat quietly with his own thoughts.

Yoshitsune's thoughts rested only for a moment on his military future. He envisioned it so clearly, he felt no need to dwell on it. Instead he reached into the folds of his sleeve to touch the fan he always carried now, the little fan of hinoki wood he had taken from Uji. Yoshitsune longed for the beautiful Kyo-no-Kimi, and touching the fan brought her image more clearly to his mind. He could almost see her lovely, pale face and her long black hair.

Then, in a sudden change of mood, Yoshitsune leaped to his feet, alert and restless once more.

"I wish to meet Saigyo," he said.

He turned at a sound behind him.

"I apologize for neglecting you," said a firm but gentle voice. "But I have been trying to find out the position of the Heike soldiers."

Yoshitsune bowed to the tall, imposing figure of the great monk who stood, staff in hand, his robes flowing around him, at the top of the path. The glance that fell on Yoshitsune shone with a mixture of spirituality and worldly intelligence.

When Yoshitsune raised his eyes to Saigyo, the look then exchanged was one full of understanding. Somehow, Yoshitsune felt, this man knew him not only for what he was but for what he would be. And he felt in the wise monk a sympathy, an understanding of the unease within, the unspoken need for love, for approval, for a belonging to something.

Saigyo bowed to Yoshitsune in return and smiled, and Yoshitsune, aware that something had happened between them, answered the unspoken thought.

"I hope we shall meet again, sir."

"I shall see to it," the older man answered calmly.

Yoshitsune felt he must admit his action earlier that morning. "I could not help but read some of the poetry on your desk, and I also listened to your morning prayers." A note of eagerness crept into his voice. "I think there is much you can teach me. Some day, after I have done the things I must do, I shall come back to this place." And then, to hide his emotion, Yoshitsune spoke quickly.

"It is still day, but it is time we were gone. By this hour, Kiyomori's soldiers should be thick as flies over these hills."

"Does it worry you?" asked Saigyo. "How shall you pass through them?"

Yoshitsune smiled.

"No, I have no fear that we shall be caught any more. We shall simply ride through them in this broad daylight as though we were Heike ourselves. We are fully armored, and with a few minor changes, our armor will look like theirs. Few of them have ever seen me or my men, so they can hardly hope to recognize our faces. If we do not run too fast nor attempt to hide, no one will question us."

The monk nodded, seeing the wisdom in what Yoshitsune planned.

When, later that day, soldiers arrived at the small mountain hut, they saw only the monk Saigyo at his prayers. For days after, the soldiers of the Heike swarmed through the Eastern Hills even beyond Shirakawa Pass, until finally they were called back to the capital. The search was finished. Yoshitsune had escaped.

# Under the Heavens

The heavy autumn winds brought the first snow, and the eleventh month had already begun. It would not be long before Yoshitsune and his small band of loyal Genji followers reached their destination, the home of Hidehira Fujiwara of Mutsu. They had crossed mountains and plains, and would soon be at the foot of the greatest mountain of all, the magnificent and beautiful Mount Fuji.

Once through Shirakawa Pass, they had not run into much a village during the day, even food was no problem since the difficulty, save the problem of foraging for food. If they passed simple villagers were only too glad to welcome such visitors.

As it was obvious they were being pursued no longer, they did not hurry. If, after traveling for a while, they reached a spot that was especially lovely, they paused for a day or two to relax and enjoy themselves.

One day they came to a forest alive with wild birds and game.

"Shall we stop for a bit?" called Kisanta. "I feel frozen to this saddle and besides, my bow arm is getting rusty."

"We shall have an archery competition," decided Yoshitsune.

Then he grinned at Benkei. "And after that, we shall try our sword arms."

Benkei laughed back. "With or without scabbards?"

They all dismounted. Roping off several trees to make a corral for the horses, the men fed and curried their mounts. Yoshitsune stared at his black stallion with satisfaction, rubbing him down with care and feeding him with his own hand. Black Lacquer nuzzled Yoshitsune. But as responsive as he was to his master, let someone else approach him and he turned into a rampaging demon. Yoshitsune found the horse's wild spirit to his taste. They suited each other perfectly, and each of them knew it. With a final pat, Yoshitsune turned to join the others. Three tents had already been put up, one for eating, one for sleeping, and the third for Yoshitsune's use alone. Brushwood was gathered, and a kettle of water set to boil for tea and to cook the rice. The trees provided excellent shelter against the wind. It would be a cosy and comfortable night.

The men removed their billowing mantles and their armor in order to move about more freely. Clad only in his snug-fitting warrior's tunic and trousers, each rebuckled on sword and dagger and slung a bow and a quiver of arrows over his shoulder. After tramping through the woods for half an hour, they came to an open clearing, perfect for an archery match.

Kisanta strode across the clearing and pointed to an unusually cleft twig on the branch of one of the trees.

"Let us begin with that, shall we?"

"By all means," called Yoshitsune.

They were all expert archers. Since the mounted archer had always been the backbone of fighting warrior forces in Japan, the utmost skill with bow and arrow was necessary. Depending on the strength and prowess of the warrior, the shafts, with eagle or falcon feathers, measured from twelve to fifteen handbreadths. A handbreadth equaled the distance from the tip of the thumb to the little finger. The arrow of a good warrior measured thirteen handbreadths, about three feet. The arrow of a great warrior measured a full fifteen handbreadths, close to four feet in length. Some of the bows stood as tall as a man.

Kisanta and Kijiro were remarkable archers. Tsugunobu and Tadanobu were good, though their skill lay primarily with the sword. The great, powerful arms of Benkei did well with any weapon he could lay his hands on. He was best in hand-to-hand combat, at which he could outreach, outlast, and outmaneuver any man alive, except Yoshitsune.

Yoshitsune himself had an uncanny, natural ability with every type of weapon. He was able to exercise perfect control over his every movement, to think out each thing before it happened. He moved so quickly mere strength could never overcome him. His horsemanship was without compare; his skill with the sword was worthy of the greatest warriors in history. He had had little experience with bow and arrow, yet he was improving under the guidance of the Yoshioka brothers. He planned to try Kisanta's mighty bow that day.

They practiced for a little over an hour before it was decided to hold the competition.

"Tsugunobu first," cried Kisanta.

Tsugunobu gave a mock groan. "That is not fair. I am no match for the rest of you."

"Fair or not," Kijiro said, "shoot away."

Tsugunobu drew an arrow from his quiver. The arrow whistled through the air, missing the tiny mark only narrowly.

"Your turn, brother," he said to Tadanobu. "See if you cannot save our honor and show these upstart Yoshiokas a thing or two."

But Tadanobu missed the tiny target as well.

"Who shall be next?" asked Kisanta.

"Since you are the master of ceremonies, you choose," declared Yoshitsune.

"Very well. Benkei."

The big man strode forward into the clearing and, choosing

a lighter bow than usual, drew back the shaft. It is doubtful whether a hair could have been fitted into the space between the target and the path of Benkei's arrow, but it had to be said that Benkei missed it, too.

"Is it permitted for my brother and me to shoot together?" demanded Kisanta.

"I don't know that it is a correct thing in a competition," said Yoshitsune, "but since the show might be worth it, let us stretch the rules a little."

The Yoshioka brothers stood side by side, and as though each were the shadow of the other, drew their shafts in a single movement. The two arrows flew through the air as though bound together in their paths by an invisible string, and together, forming a V, they hit the target.

"Bravo, bravo. *Banzai!*"

The men applauded and bowed to Kisanta and Kijiro.

"And I?" Yoshitsune stepped into the middle of the clearing, measured his paces, and said, "May I use your bow and one of your arrows?"

Kisanta smiled with pleasure and presented his weapons.

Yoshitsune flexed the heavy bow. It no longer surprised his men, as it often did strangers, how much hidden strength lay in his wiry, slender body. The muscles in his arms tightened as he drew the shaft and let it fly. Swiftly it soared through the air and plunged directly into the center of the V formed by the arrows of the Yoshioka brothers.

For a moment, the men were silent, in utter amazement. Yoshitsune had just outdone the two finest archers in Japan.

"And I was the one who taught you!" gasped Kisanta. He shook his head in mock sorrow. His feeling for Yoshitsune was too strong for envy, and pride shone in his eyes at the sight of his master's brilliant marksmanship.

Kijiro hurried to a tree beyond, on which still clung a few maple leaves. He wove them ably into a wreath, which he came

over to present to Yoshitsune.

Placing the wreath on Yoshitsune's head, he uttered solemnly, "Lord of all archers in the world."

After much merriment, they agreed it was time to stop for the evening. Should they decide to remain at the campsite, they would hold the sword competition the next day.

Yoshitsune, who always liked to be clean, set off to find a spring or pool where he might bathe. He hated the thought of going to bed without having washed. Not far from the clearing, a small brook wound its way through the forest. There he undressed and plunged into the icy water. He washed, rinsed his mouth, and cleaned his teeth with a small square of cloth. Then he returned to the tents.

Soon after, hot steamed rice, roasted rabbit, and boiling tea were ready. The men ate and sat around the fire far into the night, talking or staring at the silent stars. Later, when the fire was out, Benkei attended Yoshitsune in his tent. Wrapped warmly in heavy quilts, the men slept that night in peace.

As pleasant as the forest was, Yoshitsune was growing eager to arrive in the east. So the next morning they mounted their horses and rode on.

Late in the afternoon dark clouds loomed in the sky and the sound of thunder echoed distantly in the heavy air. A swirling wind lashed the pine trees until their tops swayed and trembled. Suddenly, a driving sleet crashed earthward, there was a blazing crack of lightning, and the afternoon darkened like the blackest night.

There was nothing to do but to push on. The horses reared, neighing loudly in their fright. Huddling together, the men urged their horses forward. They passed a shrine and knew a village could not be far off. Tadanobu rode on a little ahead and returned to report that a farmhouse lay at not too great a distance beyond.

In a few minutes they made out the dim outline of a small

dwelling. A flash of lightning illuminated the low thatched roof of the main house and those of several outbuildings and barns. The men hurried toward the house.

A cry greeted them as they rode in past the gate. Someone was waving a lantern in the courtyard to show the way, and they followed the light. The lantern led them to a stable, and as the man swung the doors open against the wind, they rode directly inside.

"What can you be thinking of, riding about on such a night!" The farmer's country accent was so thick they could barely understand his words.

When he had succeeded in closing the barn doors, the farmer turned around to look at his visitors. His face grew pale, and his jaw hung open. He had supposed his visitors to be neighbors returning from the village. Now that he saw them more clearly in their shining armor and billowing silken mantles, he was too stunned by such illustrious company to speak. Overcome with awe, he fell to his knees and knocked his head against the earth in obeisance.

"We apologize for coming on you like this," said Yoshitsune gently, moved by the poor man's distress. "If you would be so kind as to let us stay in this stable until the storm passes, we should be most grateful."

The gentle and kindly tones of Yoshitsune's voice confused the farmer even more. He was hardly used to being spoken to so gently by such great lords. He would have been less confused if Yoshitsune had commanded him harshly.

There seemed to be no way to pull the farmer out of his trance, so the men attended to the horses themselves, feeding them and rubbing them down. Then Benkei walked over to the farmer, who still lay trembling on the ground, and touched him gently on the shoulder.

"We shall manage well enough here," he said, "and so will our retainers when they catch up with us. But I would be grateful if you brought my lord to the main house and saw to his comfort. He cannot spend the night in this dismal barn."

Finally, the man scrambled to his feet and stuttered a humble invitation to the band to enter his poor house, where he would do everything in his power to make them comfortable for the night. He threw all of his scant weight against the barn door, but it would not budge. When Benkei opened it with a single thrust, the farmer almost collapsed once more in his embarrassment. Somehow, at last they managed to reach the porch of the little dwelling, with the farmer bobbing his head, wringing his hands, and apologizing every step of the way.

Yoshitsune saw that the house was really one large room with a lean-to shed in back for the bath. Rush mats lay scattered about the wooden floor. There was only a small charcoal brazier for warmth. The family's few clothes hung on wooden pegs, and in one box were what quilts and rice pillows they had for bedding. But there were flowers in the alcove, and a Buddha image and the Seven Gods of Luck on the Buddha shelf.

The men were invited to sit near the room's only piece of furniture, a small, low table. In the dim light, they did not notice the rest of the family at first, huddling in the shadows of a far corner. But when the woman noticed her husband's panic, she moved forward on her knees and bowed, welcoming the men quietly. Then she shooed the children from sight and brought dry clothing, placing it on the floor before the men.

"We have very poor food, but there is enough for all. May I be permitted to prepare a little supper?"

"You are most kind," said Yoshitsune graciously. "I cannot apologize enough for putting you to all this trouble. Please know that we are grateful for your hospitality."

The woman blushed. She was not used to such courtly speech.

The men changed into the dry kimonos behind a screen, and the farmer brought rice wine. When Yoshitsune invited the farmer to sit with them, he finally began to seem a little more at ease. Yoshitsune's chatting had had a soothing effect. He had come to understand the peasants during his monastery days when he had roamed the countryside. The patience with which they accepted their hard lives moved him. They leveled their little pieces of ground; sowed the rice seeds in the early spring; guarded the tiny shoots against insects, floods, and typhoons; and then, when the Fujiwaras finished taxing them seven-tenths of their rice, there was hardly enough to feed their families for the next winter. Yoshitsune vowed not to let it go on much longer. He wondered how the farmer felt about his life and questioned him.

"It is the will of Buddha that I should work hard in this life. But it will pass. Everything passes," said the farmer quietly.

# Mountain Against the Sky

Yoshitsune rose with the dawn, and having rewarded the overjoyed farmer, he and his men mounted their horses. They accepted gladly the several days' provisions given them by the farmer's wife, and after warm and courteous farewells, continued their journey eastward.

As they rode, the country grew more mountainous.

"Soon you will see something that will take your breath away, my lord," commented Tsugunobu.

"You mean Mount Fuji," guessed Yoshitsune. It excited and pleased him to see so much of his country.

Tsugunobu nodded.

A few hours later, they were winding their way up the steep slopes of the foothills. Tsugunobu bent close to Yoshitsune and whispered, "Ride on ahead to the top of the hill, and you will be the first to see it."

Yoshitsune smiled and urged on his horse.

From the top of the hill, he looked down into the waters of a great lake, calm and glinting with sunlight. And there, reflected in the clear waters was the glorious image. It was best to look at the image in the water first, to prepare for the mountain itself. Slowly, Yoshitsune raised his eyes to the full force of the grandeur, the unsurpassable beauty of Fujiyama. The mountain was a perfect cone. Its slopes swept upward to the snow-capped peak, which seemed to pierce the heavens. They stared at each other for a long time—the greatness of the mountain and the growing greatness of the young lord, each with his own beauty, his own majestic grandeur.

Standing there, facing that mountain, Yoshitsune understood the meaning of final peace. He was not ready for peace yet. But one day the time would come. Yoshitsune bowed low to the mountain as the others rode up in silence, each in his own way marveling at Mount Fuji.

Then they rode around the ridge above the lake, following Yoshitsune as he led them on and beyond to the north, until Mount Fuji lay behind them and night closed in, hiding all but the mountain's dark outline from view.

At Mutsu, Hidehira Fujiwara sat in the main hall of his great manor house. From the matted dais raised a little above the level of the floor, he watched the ten chief warriors he had invited to his midday banquet. As they ate and talked, Hidehira's shrewd eyes examined each of them, rating their strength, merit, loyalty. The purpose of the banquet was more than just another entertainment. It was the beginning of a plan that had been carefully thought out by the two greatest chieftains of the east, himself and Tokimasa of the Hojo. The original idea, however, had not been theirs. It had come from the subtle, cool, and politically brilliant mind of a far younger yet far greater man—Yoritomo of the Genji. The three of them, Hidehira, Tokimasa, and Yoritomo, were in complete agreement.

This friendship had not been sudden. It had happened slowly, as Yoritomo had grown up among them and influenced them. None of the eastern lords had been pleased with the political situation for a long time, but it was Yoritomo who had united and led them.

A second important event was the escape of Yoshitsune. Yoritomo did not consider his brother's escape very important yet, but Hidehira himself was overjoyed—partly because it further unified their forces, and partly because he would very much like to have seen his old rival Kiyomori's face when it happened. He was anxious to see Yoshitsune and waited for him with eager curiosity.

But at the moment Hidehira had a job to do, and he turned his attention back to the feasting warriors. He had given strict orders that the wine jugs were to be kept full and that his guests were to be made relaxed and comfortable. He had something to tell his warriors, and he wanted to test their reactions when they were off guard. Sober and prepared, they would of course be loyal. But Hidehira wanted to be surer of them than that.

By midafternoon, he judged the moment ripe. He reached for the wine jug and refilled the cups of those seated nearest to him.

Then he said casually, "Yoshitsune of the Genji, son of Yoshitomo and youngest brother of Yoritomo, has escaped from Heike captivity. I expect him here soon. He will be my guest."

There was a murmur of approval. But Hidehira expected that much. These eastern Heike and Fujiwara lords did not like their courtly cousins. Their interests were much closer to those of the Genji clan. But how far would they support the Genji against their own families? That was what Hidehira had to find out.

"You know, of course, that the struggle between the Heike and the Genji is not over. Kiyomori may have won the Hogen and Heiji wars, but he has not improved the country. He and Goshirakawa do all they can to take away our prestige and our lands. It is no secret that the country is being starved of its wealth to support the pleasures of the capital."

Hidehira breathed deeply. Then he said what was most important in his quietest voice.

"Tokimasa of the Hojo, cousin clan to the Heike, and I, general-in-chief of Kiyomori's Heike and Fujiwara forces in the east appointed by Kiyomori himself, have pledged our support to Yoritomo of the Genji when he shall raise the white banner once more against the Heike of Kyoto."

A great hush filled the hall. Then into the silence came a roar of voices. Hidehira glanced quickly from one face to the other. There could be no doubt. They were with him to the last warrior. One after the other, the men bowed before him and pledged themselves, their families, their resources, and all their retainers to his service whenever the time should come.

Hidehira Fujiwara, member of one of the most ancient and noble families of the land, rarely showed his pleasure. Proud, stern, and dignified, Hidehira for the first time in many years actually smiled. He leaned back against his cushions and motioned with his hand for the feast to continue. The men grew noisier than ever with the joy of the coming conflict. At last they did not have to sit idly by, but would be called upon to fight for their lands and their privileges. Nothing could have pleased them more. Their devotion to Hidehira alone would have carried the day, but that he should have chosen to fight for what they also believed in gave the warriors an enormous satisfaction.

The shadows were beginning to deepen. A sharp, chill wind carried the faint memory of salt from the sea not many miles away. The wild countryside was rugged and strong.

Yoshitsune felt the strength of the land and its people with sudden intensity, and his heart surged in response. His eyes swept across the horizon, across the fields and the hillocks to the distant mountains. Without completely taming it, the people had nevertheless made the land work for them. They did not huddle together in a single village, but scattered themselves in groups of three and four houses on their lands. The solid huts, with thatched roofs and wide-spreading gables, stood their ground

proudly, keeping guard over fields of barley and millet, over rice
paddies, over hilly timberland. And the peasants did not look
hopeless or exhausted like the peasants in the west.

In the hills beyond, built to command a view of all its domains,
lay the manor house of Lord Hidehira Fujiwara. In the deepen-
ing dusk, Yoshitsune and his band of Genji rode forward.
Yoshitsune could only guess at his reception, though it was
understood that this was where he was to go.

At the foot of the slopes were storehouses and barns. They
contained enough produce to feed the entire population should
the crops fail. Everywhere could be seen a firm and wisely
controlled organization. Yoshitsune was struck by the extent of
his brother's skill and knowledge, knowing it was Yoritomo who
had brought such strength and order to the east.

Tadanobu and Tsugunobu, who alone were familiar with
the place, led the way along the rocky trail upward through the
pine and bamboo forest. Here and there were flowerbeds, rock

gardens, a small pavilion—all arranged by someone who knew how to work with, not against, the natural beauty of the forest. Below them, they could see the plains, where the wild, swift horses of the Kanto were bred and trained, where warriors practiced or rode off to hunt with their hawks. Above, on the ridge, the pagoda of a temple was outlined against the sky.

Yoshitsune gloried in the immensity of it all, as he rode in his splendid armor, the crest of the Genji upon his helmet, the white banner held aloft in his hand, through the gates into the presence of Hidehira Fujiwara. There, Yoshitsune saw at once that not only Hidehira but his warriors as well had gathered in front of the great central hall to greet him. He sat tall on his horse and carried himself proudly.

Nearer the house Yoshitsune dismounted, and motioning to his followers to accompany him, approached Hidehira, who greeted him warmly. It was the greeting of one leader of men to another.

"So, he has arrived, has he."

The cool, even bluntness of the voice no longer startled Tokimasa of the Hojo as it had years before. In the fourteen years since Yoritomo had first come, the warm, intelligent old nobleman had almost grown used to the impenetrable quality of Yoritomo's nature. Almost, but not quite.

There was no question of Tokimasa's belief in Yoritomo. Quite the contrary. He recognized in Yoritomo a supremacy, an unquestionable and unquestioned capacity to command and shape the destiny of a country. It was more than the power to lead other men. It was the power to foresee events; to mold neither underreach nor would he overreach himself, and there them. It was a power like the power of the gods. He would was no possibility at all that he would not succeed.

Yet with this nature was an utter detachment. Inside Yoritomo stirred no feeling or emotion. He was like the stillness of the heavens, the dispassionate calm of a windless sea. His was a mind with no disturbing echoes, no shadowy afterthoughts, only clarity and absolute logic.

Yoritomo was a law unto himself. He had no ordinary scruples, but obeyed his own moral code.

Having just left Yoshitsune, Tokimasa could not help comparing the two brothers. Both were strong, courageous, and able to command. But their characters were as different as possible. The wild, impetuous emotionalism of Yoshitsune, the fiery heat of his nature, his intense loves and hates, his restlessness, his sensitivity to whatever was about him—Tokimasa smiled. It would be a most interesting moment when the two brothers came face to face.

"He is very anxious to see you," urged Tokimasa.

"Not for the time being," said Yoritomo.

Once again, Tokimasa could not help comparing the two. He remembered the expressive features of the younger brother and contrasted them with the almost immovable features of the elder. Thirteen years between them, Yoshitsune sixteen, Yoritomo twenty-nine—yet far more separated them than years.

"He will be disappointed."

Yoritomo looked away. "Then he must be disappointed. It is not wise that we should meet as yet. There is still much to prepare before the time is ripe. A meeting would stir up too much enthusiasm among the warriors, and they are already overanxious to begin battle. Our meeting will be the sound of the bell. It is the thing they are waiting for, the signal. And since we are not yet ready, it must wait."

"Will you write to him? Will you tell him this?"

"You will tell him for me."

Tokimasa sighed. He remembered the hope in Yoshitsune's eyes. He had waited long and traveled far to join his brother. Yet Yoshitsune would understand.

"A secret meeting perhaps?"

"Surely that is not necessary," said Yoritomo coldly.

Tokimasa would not have been afraid to repeat his request. He did not fear Yoritomo's impatience since he had never known him to lose patience. But he also knew that Yoritomo never changed his mind unless new facts changed the circumstances. Such advice as he considered wise, he accepted immediately, for he knew better than to refuse wise counsel. Yet on this matter, he had made a decision, and barring unforeseen circumstances, his decision was final.

The two men had been sitting in Yoritomo's private rooms in the eastern wing of Tokimasa's mansion. Yoritomo occupied his old rooms there when he was not in his own house several miles away at Kamakura.

A moment later one of the doors slid open. Tokimasa knew who it was even without looking around. Only one person in the world could disturb Yoritomo without requesting an audience, even without knocking.

"How are you, father?" The clear, girlish voice rang through the air, fresh and happy as the morning. "Since I am quite certain I am disturbing you, I won't make any needless apologies."

Tokimasa shook his head wryly. Since the day she had eloped with Yoritomo, Masako had spoken and lived almost with the freedom of a man. Old-fashioned, used to the shyness of his own wife, Tokimasa could not help but wonder at this remarkable daughter of his. It was partly that she had been brought up so far from the etiquette of court, partly her own strength of character. But mostly it was that Yoritomo chose to have her this way. He enjoyed her company. He trusted her completely. And Tokimasa thought secretly Yoritomo was grooming her to take his place should anything happen to him. Strange that he should choose a woman, yet it seemed Yoritomo trusted her ability more than those of the men around him. And insofar as he was capable of affection for any human, Yoritomo loved her.

"Without meaning to distress you," said Yoritomo, "I am forced to admit that you did not disturb us in the least. I know how much you enjoy provoking me."

"Nothing provokes you, nothing at all." She smiled at her father. "Though I do my best."

Tokimasa enjoyed seeing them together. When Masako was with him, Yoritomo came closest to being relaxed, almost warm.

After a pleasant luncheon, Yoritomo called for his maps, and a serious discussion of campaigns and the training of warriors began. It lasted for several hours.

The perfection of his plans, the brilliance of the way he used his resources, could not but impress Tokimasa. Yoritomo's knowledge of what was happening in every corner of Japan was incredibly accurate.

Noting Tokimasa's amazement, Yoritomo commented, "My Tengu have done well, have they not?"

"Even the demons of the mountains have bestowed their favor on you," smiled Tokimasa. "How can you not succeed?"

# Genji

"Your brother thinks it wise that you should not meet for a while."

Hidehira caught Yoshitsune's quick flush.

"I see," answered Yoshitsune. "I suppose he has some definite reason."

"You'll discover that Yoritomo never does anything without careful thought," said Hidehira. "I have had a note from him in which he sends you his warmest greetings. His feeling is that until all is ready, a meeting between the two of you would only enflame the warriors. They are already too excited about marching west against the capital."

Yoshitsune was disappointed that after his long journey he was not to stand before his brother, to be admitted to his confidence and service. He did understand Yoritomo's reasoning. And yet, studying the veiled eyes of Hidehira, Yoshitsune wondered if there were not more to the delay than the reason given.

But he said merely, "And in the meantime?"

Hidehira sighed as for now at least, Yoshitsune agreed. "We had a long discussion about you," he said.

"So?"

"He wanted to know all about you. He has something definite he wants you to do. He wanted to know whether I thought you capable."

Yoshitsune stood up and threw back the shutters. The late winter afternoon sun shone pale and brought no warmth. It glittered on the bare branches of the frozen garden, where only the ageless pine tree kept its color. They were sitting in the small mountain lodge that Hidehira had given to Yoshitsune. He had guessed rightly that Yoshitsune would be more comfortable there than in the guest wing of the manor house.

Yoshitsune loved the solitude and the wilderness of his forest lodge. It was as if the entire mountain were his own garden. The lodge was simply furnished and in perfect taste. Except for two or three kitchen servants, he kept only his small band with him. It was a good thing, Yoshitsune decided, that he was happy in the lodge. It looked as if the quarters were to be more permanent than he had expected.

Yoshitsune waited for Hidehira to continue.

"I won't embarrass you by repeating the conversation," said Hidehira, the trace of a smile in his deep-set eyes. "I shall merely inform you that you are to be a commander in Yoritomo's army. If you accept the appointment, there is much work to be done."

"I had assumed as much on both counts," answered Yoshitsune.

Hidehira nodded. "That is as it should be."

"How many men does Yoritomo want? What men may I count upon?"

Yoshitsune's quick grasp of the situation obviously startled Hidehira. Yoshitsune was amused. And he noted that Hidehira's reply was thoughtful and practical.

"On the day you arrived, I gave a banquet for the chief warriors in the east. Their loyalty is firm. Their interests are ours, and you may count on them completely. Their individual skill is great, but they aren't yet disciplined as a fighting force.

They are wilder and less easy to handle than the country lords near Kyoto. But if you gain their loyalty, as you have that of your own followers, they will be the heart of a powerful army."

"And their retainers? How do they number?"

"Each of the ten warriors can count on about thirty retainers. Since Yoritomo desires an army of five hundred men, there are still two hundred to recruit," answered Hidehira.

"How will the farmers submit to this?"

"Shall you leave them much choice?" asked Hidehira.

Yoshitsune smiled. "Good. Then we are ready to begin. I would like to meet with the chief warriors as soon as possible."

Hidehira did not question the authority Yoshitsune put in his voice, and the young leader was glad. He knew that his bearing and tone must command obedience if he were to succeed in spite of his youth. He felt certain now that Hidehira would give his support, his experience, and all his men and horses for him to use as he thought best.

And with such plans and preparations the New Year passed. And then another year, and another winter turned into spring. It was the beginning of the third month, and already the plum blossoms were beginning to fall and those of the peach and the pear to bloom. The willows on the banks of the mountain rivers showed a faint tinge of green, and in the morning, the spring mist trailed across the mountains and through the trees.

Benkei, Kisanta, and Kijiro, in the headiness of the spring air, had been unable to resist planting a garden around the lodge. One day Yoshitsune returned from the archery training field to find that just outside his rooms a rock pool had been built, and that the men had planted peony, azalea, and wisteria beneath his window. It was beautiful.

As Yoshitsune came upon them while they were working, the three stood up embarrassed.

"Thank you," Yoshitsune said simply.

"It was really much too bare," grumbled Benkei, trying to hide his confusion.

Kisanta and Kijiro laughed, their handsome faces reflecting the happiness they felt at giving their leader pleasure. Kijiro said, "It is all very well to be rustic, but some refinements are pleasant."

Kisanta sighed. "We tried to get that barbaric Tadanobu to help, but one cannot tear him away from his war maps and horses these days."

Yoshitsune gloried once again, as he often had in months past, in these five men, his own band. Their loyalty, their experience, their various skills had been and were important to him—Benkei, who so often stood between him and his own temper; Tadanobu, whose years of mountain roving had taught him about guerrilla fighting; Kisanta and Kijiro, who were not only gay company but extremely able warriors; and Tsugunobu, whose spiritual strength and quiet knowledge of the ways of men and the gods had opened new thresholds for Yoshitsune's thoughts to cross. He well knew their worth.

By now they lived in different houses. Kisanta and Kijiro each had a mistress and had built small dwellings on the lower slope so that their parties would not disturb anyone. Tsugunobu and Tadanobu lived closer, in a tiny pavilion they had designed themselves. Yet the bond between them all remained unbroken.

The months had passed quickly in rounds of archery practice, the training and mastering of horses, increasing skill with the long sword and dagger, and the building up of physical endurance. All of this was extremely necessary. Since they were far outnumbered by the Heike, the Genji forces had to have greater skill and the ability to last longer in battle. Under Yoshitsune's generalship the various clan forces had become a unified army, and he had made them understand that the old way of fighting as separate bands would serve only to exhaust their energies. He had taught them the need for tactical maneuvers, working as parts of a single unit under a single leadership, instead of plunging helter-skelter at the enemy with unthinking courage.

"I have been considering a new type of maneuver," said Yoshitsune as they sat down to a supper of raw fish and rice and the first fruits of the year.

"You think of almost nothing else," muttered Benkei, still the only one who could say whatever he pleased to his master without being afraid.

Yoshitsune rose and paced restlessly about the room. "We are so nearly ready," he said, flushing with anger. "How much longer will it be? How long must we wait? It has been months."

The men who sat about him glanced up with sympathy. They understood what was troubling him most.

"Why does Yoritomo keep me waiting! He has sent no message for weeks. I understood his reasons for not welcoming me in person right away, but surely this is too much."

Yoshitsune's eyes flared. "As my elder brother and chief of our clan I accept his authority and decision in such matters. I owe him my loyalty and obedience, but it is all getting extremely difficult. He asked for an army. I have provided him with one. He asked that they be well trained. With few exceptions, I will answer for each horseman and foot soldier. It has been a year and a half now since we came, and still nothing has happened. What is he waiting for?"

Several months later, as the torrential rains of early summer lashed the sea into a fury and the wind beat the waves against the rocky coast, Yoritomo sat in the central hall of his house. He was at Kamakura. Gathered around him were Hidehira Fujiwara, Tokimasa of the Hojo, and two of his finest generals. Also there were three of his Tengu who had lately arrived from the west—Goro, Adachi, and Kawata. If any of them had wondered at the delay in attacking the Heike forces, Yoritomo soon made his reasons abundantly clear.

"There is no question of the fact that we are ready," he began briefly. "It is the moment, the time that is not right. Since we are far outnumbered, we must use every asset we have. One of these assets is time."

"What can time accomplish that large armies cannot?" demanded Tokimasa, who, like the generals, was impatient. "Such time is also on their side. Surely they know by now at least some of what is going on here, and with time, they too can train their soldiers to greater efficiency."

"There are two major errors in what you have just said," answered Yoritomo in his cool, flat voice. "First of all, though I am sure the court is aware of our discontent, it can have no knowledge at all of my particular plans." He nodded in the direction of the three Tengu. "We have excellent sources of information. Secondly, there are two things working against the more efficient training of their army. The Heike have spent so many years among the luxuries and corrupting pleasures of Kyoto, they have wasted so much energy on petty court intrigues and palace factions, that they are by now unfit for military life. One day out in the field, and their generals will fold up in discomfort. They have committed the stupidest of all mistakes. They have cut themselves off from the land, and it is from the land that our strength comes. Instead of increasing their power and their prestige, they have sowed discontent and misery among the people, who hate them now. And worse, they have sucked their wealth without increasing its source. They have reaped their harvest without planting new crops."

"You mentioned another factor," urged Hidehira.

"I understand Kiyomori," said Yoritomo softly. "I was already fourteen before I left Kyoto, and during the time I was kept prisoner on his estate, I learned much about him. And I have learned even more watching what has happened since. It would be to his advantage now to attack us first. But Kiyomori will never begin a battle. He gets sick at the very thought of bloodshed. I do not condemn him for his desire for peace. It is the ultimate goal of us all. But I pity him his lack of foresight. There are many wrongs in the land that must be righted before the country is at rest; and if bloodshed is necessary to accomplish this end, then so be it. Kiyomori has won only a temporary peace. I think he knows it, but either cannot or will not act on his knowledge. It shall be his undoing.

"And so time is our ally, and not theirs. Our strength shall increase as they grow weaker."

"Is there more?" questioned Hidehira.

"A third and last point," said Yoritomo. "The attitude of the two powerful monasteries at Mount Hiei and Nara. I will not pretend that they are our allies. But they are angry still at Kiyomori and the Heike for having beaten them fifteen years ago when the monastic armies marched on Kyoto. Besides, their interests are closer to ours. Since Kiyomori has been in power, he has begun to take, here a little, there a little, and give the land back to the imperial court. No, the monasteries are not happy with Kiyomori, and I think they will offer us their assistance, or at least their support." Yoritomo smiled. "Also, I have sent money to Nara for the rebuilding of temples."

The men nodded. As always, Yoritomo had foreseen the future much more clearly than they.

"There is something else I wish to say." Yoritomo's tone commanded silence. "When the battle is over and done, I shall not establish the government in Kyoto."

If it came as something of a shock that Yoritomo already considered himself the head of the new government, it was a shock that was only mildly felt. After all, the eastern lords had left matters in Yoritomo's hands for so long, that not only would it be almost impossible for them to unseat his authority, but they had no wish to do so. He was their rightful leader by virtue of being the greatest among them. What was more, they trusted his wisdom and his just nature.

"I will establish the government here in Kamakura because it will be much wiser to keep away from the luxuries of the court. We in this room would not be affected, but ordinary men grow soft living in Kyoto."

"What about the emperor?" questioned Hidehira.

"The emperor is Japan's sacred heritage from the gods. He is part of the soul of our people and will be protected. The imperial court, the Fujiwara nobles, and the monasteries will keep the lands and the income that are rightfully theirs. But corruption will come to an end. Officials will do their duties or be banished. Lords will return to their estates and no longer neglect their peasants or their lands." Yoritomo paused and then added calmly, "I will see justice and order in Japan."

"So be it," murmured Hidehira.

"We are with you to the last," applauded Tokimasa.

When the audience ended and the others left, Yoritomo turned to his three Tengu.

"You have done well, my demons," he said. "You have brought me news worth hearing, and you handled my brother's escape admirably. Fly back now, and continue as you have been."

Goro bowed, and drawing his hooded cloak about him, led the others from the room.

It was a year and a half later, the autumn of 1178. Little had happened to disturb the continued calm of Yoshitsune and his men at Mutsu, save for the marriage of Kisanta Yoshioka to the niece of one of the eastern lords.

It was late in the afternoon, and the sunset fired the autumn tints to exquisite loveliness. Returning from an all-day hawk hunt with his companions, Yoshitsune approached his lodge feeling more restless than usual. Shortly after he had retired to his room and had changed from his rough hunting cloak to a suit of soft white silk, Benkei brought a note to him. It was written on thick dark paper and the handwriting was of such unusual perfection and dignity that Yoshitsune desired immediately to see its owner. Benkei pointed silently to a figure standing motionless in the garden. The figure was robed in flowing priestly garments, and at the sound of Yoshitsune's voice, it turned and bowed deeply. The craggy features, the piercing eyes were unmistakable.

"Saigyo!" Yoshitsune cried out. "What a welcome sight you are. I had long given up hope that you would keep your promise. Please come in. Benkei, order some supper for us all."

Saigyo smiled at the warmth in Yoshitsune's welcome. Slowly he ascended the wooden steps onto the veranda and stepped into the room.

Through the evening they spoke of one thing and another, Yoshitsune testing on this very wisest of men the thoughts and ideas that had been forming in his mind.

Later on Yoshitsune asked almost shyly, "Will you play for me? It has been a long time since I have heard music save for my own, which I must admit is not very good."

Saigyo nodded and called for a native zithern. He tuned it to a difficult mode. Yoshitsune accompanied him quite nicely on the flute, and they passed a pleasant evening. As Yoshitsune rose to guide his guest to his room, he paused, speaking hesitantly.

"You travel freely and must therefore hear occasional scraps of all sorts of news. I wonder . . . have you recently heard news from the Imperial Palace? I do not speak of politics, only of the happenings at court. Oh well," he said suddenly. "Never mind. The matter is of no importance."

Saigyo smiled. "Many months ago I received a note from your devoted Benkei. Among other things, he asked me to bring a certain piece of information should I manage to journey here to the east."

Yoshitsune's heart flooded with gratitude toward his faithful retainer. "And have you heard anything?"

"Kyo-no-Kimi is not yet married and remains in the empress's service. More than that I do not know, except that a betrothal arranged by her father was broken some time ago."

Saigyo rested his hand lightly on Yoshitsune's shoulder. "I have heard great things of you, how your men love and respect you, how you are just in thought and deed, of your bravery, of your supreme intelligence, and even of your excellence in the military arts." Saigyo smiled. "But I have also heard of your still violent temper and your impulsiveness and of the anger that you bear your brother."

"I have served his interests well," said Yoshitsune coldly, withdrawing under Saigyo's close scrutiny.

"I'm sorry," said Saigyo quickly. "I did not mean to intrude in your affairs."

Yoshitsune's expression softened as swiftly as it had grown hard. "You have the right. I don't know why, but ever since that day when I met you in your mountain retreat, I have felt a kinship to you. There is much you can teach me, and I thank you for your interest in my welfare."

"I knew your father well," commented Saigyo. "You are like him in many ways. He was a friend to me, and if ever you need me, depend on it, I shall be there."

Yoshitsune clenched his hands. "He shall be revenged soon, and my mother."

"Patience," whispered Saigyo. "The time will come. And trust Yoritomo more." Saigyo paused.

"You are a priest," said Yoshitsune wonderingly. "You cannot approve of what we are preparing to do."

"War is insanity, and as a priest I cannot but believe it is an evil. And yet I do believe also that Yoritomo is the only man alive capable of ruling this land with justice. The people live in misery. Something must be done. I do not say that in Yoritomo's place I should choose to accomplish it in the way he has planned . . ." and Saigyo smiled, "but then neither am I sure that I should be so successful as he shall be."

"As for the other matter," said Yoshitsune, "do you know that I have been here nearly three years, and that never once have I laid eyes on my elder brother?"

"He has seen you," said Saigyo slowly. "And he approves."

At Kamakura, Yoritomo was strolling through the late autumn garden with his wife Masako. They were finishing a conversation which had begun many hours before.

"And now, if anything should happen to me, you will know what to do." Yoritomo turned and looked fully into his wife's face.

Without the annoying protests that he might have expected from another woman, Masako answered firmly, "Yes, I shall know what to do. With the help of my father and brother, I shall act as regent until our son has attained a manful age and shall keep the government here, away from the capital."

"I shall ask the emperor to make the title of Shogun hereditary.

You must let no one take our son's heritage."

Masako understood the warning.

"You are a remarkable woman," commented Yoritomo.

Masako's eyes sparkled. "Why else would you have married me?"

A messenger interrupted them to announce to Yoritomo that a visitor awaited him in the eastern wing.

"His name?"

"Yoshinaka of the Genji."

Yoritomo sent in the message that he would be there presently.

"My cousin," he said. "The son of my father's brother Yoshikata. My eldest brother, among those executed by Kiyomori, killed Yoshikata many years ago in a family quarrel. After the Heiji War, Yoshinaka was carried away into the mountains where he was brought up in hiding by Genji retainers. I sent for him to join us here if he were so minded."

"What is he like, your cousin Yoshinaka?"

"I have heard a few extremely varied reports. It seems I shall have to make up my own mind."

"But then you always do," said Masako.

# The Genji Rise Again

To herald the spring after a long and gloomy winter, Yoshitsune had decided to hold a grand festival, the main event of which was to be a horse race. Although the strictness of everyday life in the east suited him well, he longed every now and then for a more elaborate entertainment. Accordingly, preparations had been started months before for both the horse race and the festivities that were to follow it.

He had sought out the greatest masters in the art of forging, and since the New Year they had been hard at work, fashioning the finest swords and armor. Disregarding Yoritomo's strict rules about a warrior's mode of dress, Yoshitsune had ordered new robes and undertunics to be made from silks and brocades for all his men, and even the common foot soldiers received bolts of excellent cloth.

Along the racing grounds pavilions had been built for the contestants and their grooms, and from their pinnacles gaily colored pennants flashed and rippled in the spring breezes. Stands and platforms had been raised for the musicians and for those who were not taking part in the race, and a long galley had been fenced off for the throngs of peasants who were

93

coming from all over eastern Japan for the unusual event.

Horses and riders had been training and preparing for months. A master of ceremonies had been chosen, Kijiro Yoshioka, to arrange for the sequence of events, to see to the musicians, and to organize the banquet and other entertainments that were to follow.

"I, for one," commented Tokimasa, "could not be more pleased. Court life, with this sort of thing going on all the time, would irritate me. But I must admit that on occasion, festivities such as this are very pleasant. It reminds one that one is still civilized enough to appreciate luxuries."

Hidehira agreed. "I, too, would not wish to live in the constant display of the imperial court. Yet I cannot see why we need avoid pleasures altogether."

Benkei, however, was highly disturbed. "It is not that I am against festivities," he grumbled. "But I have a feeling your brother is going to come crashing down on your head. You know how he detests anything that reminds him of the degenerate elegance of the court. I heard only the other day how he slashed the clothes from one of his warriors because he thought them too elaborate. When he talks of the simple austerity of a warrior's life, he means it."

Yoshitsune's mouth curved in a wry smile. "My reasons for doing this are very simple. For one thing, I feel like it. My brother's code is all very well, but I refuse to give up pleasure simply out of fear of becoming soft. For another, it just might bring Yoritomo crashing down on my head, as you put it. If I must outrage him in order to meet him, then that is exactly what I intend to do."

"Danger is your best friend," groaned Benkei. "Sense is something you were just not born with."

The morning of the race dawned brilliant and clear. The cherry blossoms had recently fallen, and the green turf displayed scattered carpets of shining pink and white. Trees proudly lifted new leaves, and the air was filled with the fragrance of flowers.

The announcing of the day's entries was done with pleasing ritual and the music began. Yoshitsune glanced at the stands where the elder warriors were excitedly discussing the various merits of each entry. He watched the crowds of jostling farmers and their families who lined the race course. He saw that the physicians stood in readiness near the tilting field. Not far from the pavilions was the paddock, where impatient racehorses pawed the air.

In another moment, Kijiro would announce the opening tournament. Grooms were rushing about readying the horses and riders, with their helmets, banners, and the long poles for the jousting matches that were to be held after the races. With a sense of satisfaction, Yoshitsune reflected that the whole scene was quite equal to the splendor and excitement of the races at court. He hurried to take his place in the lists.

Event followed event, and the morning passed swiftly. The roar of the crowds swelled with the pounding of hooves on the green turf. Thunderous applause echoed the rolling of drums as each race ended and the victor was proclaimed. The air shook with the burst of applause as Yoshitsune raced the glorious Black Lacquer to victory against a worthy chestnut. The warriors flew on their horses in a superb exhibition of horsemanship, and the valley walls hurled back the turbulent shouting.

But the greatest excitement was yet to come, the jousting matches. Yoshitsune had arranged it so that no one knew who his opponent was until one was vanquished and the helmets removed. As each pair tore down the field, jousting poles ready, the crowd screamed its approval, and the music rose in crescendo.

On a wooded hillock overlooking the valley, four men

watched the entire panorama from their horses. It would have been impossible to guess their identities, since all were dressed exactly alike, entirely in black, with neither crest nor banner to proclaim them.

"He rides brilliantly," commented one.

"What is more important, he has trained every single one of his warriors to do nearly as well. He shines like a star among them, and it is quite obvious that they worship him," said another.

"Did you see that? Remarkable performance."

"I find that Yoshitsune's name appears next after this one on the lists. I think I shall replace the man who is to be his opponent."

The speaker's declaration went unquestioned, and the four wheeled their horses about and descended into the valley.

The crowd thrilled with anticipation as they watched Yoshitsune move into position at one end of the field. Black Lacquer pranced impatiently, but steadied under his master's hand. Yoshitsune wore silver armor laced with red, and on his helmet was the white plume of the Genji. Benkei stood by his side and saw that, as always, the small fan of hinoki wood was tucked into his sleeve.

The sudden quiet of the crowd made Yoshitsune look up sharply. He saw its cause immediately. In place of one of his own colorfully attired warriors, there awaited as his opponent a strange and unknown warrior, masked and fitted out entirely in black on a snow white mount. But the drums had already begun to roll, Kijiro had announced the event, and there was no time to inquire into the matter without halting the joust and creating a stir.

Yoshitsune therefore made ready, and at the signal thundered down the field toward his unknown opponent. That the black warrior was no ordinary match was noticeable from the first moments. Though Yoshitsune plunged with all his strength, he

was unable to unseat his rival at the first pass. They turned and once again tore down the field, meeting almost head on. Yoshitsune saw that he had wounded the black warrior slightly, as his left arm hung stiffly.

Again and again, the two came on. And again and again, neither was able to unseat the other. Their mounts foamed at the mouth, and the men panted, nearly exhausted. The crowds were quiet, until the stillness roared louder than the loudest noise. And still, no one had the slightest inkling of the identity of the warrior in black. Half an hour went by. Silently, grimly, the men charged, each of them wounded slightly, each unwilling to surrender. And then, quickly, surprisingly, just as it was all growing unbearable, Yoshitsune, his blood seething with impatience and fury at the strange intruder, spun sharply and made a great plunge.

The throngs screamed with joy as the warrior in black was thrown from his horse. And they cheered when they saw Yoshitsune dismount, unwilling to take advantage of the situation on his horse. In hand to hand combat they fought, without weapons, grappling, coming apart, closing, both on the verge of collapse.

And in the next moment the warrior in black drew several feet back and held up his hand. He bowed deeply to signify his acknowledgment of Yoshitsune's victory. Benkei and the Sato brothers rushed from their pavilion to Yoshitsune's side. At the same time, three warriors in black rushed to their champion.

Yoshitsune returned the bow. "You have battled honorably and well," he said. "May I have the pleasure of knowing the name of such a worthy opponent? Surely you are a man of some great stature."

Yoshitsune's courtesy was applauded, and all turned to the unknown stranger to see what sort of response he would make.

The stranger waited a moment, and then swiftly removed his helmet and mask. The onlookers, who were aware of what had happened, gasped. For a minute Yoshitsune was uncertain. The face was one he did not remember having seen before. And then, suddenly sure, he performed a most gracious and respectful bow.

There was no doubt in his mind. He had just done battle with his brother Yoritomo and won.

It was nearing the end of 1179. Yoritomo had installed Yoshitsune beside him, and together with Yoshinaka, they firmly united the clan of the Genji and their eastern allies. The time was not far off when the rebellion would be brought into the open. Yoshitsune and Yoshinaka fretted at the delay.

Yoshitsune paid his elder brother and chieftain every respect and form of obedience. Yoritomo responded with every civility. Yet it could not be said there was much evidence of brotherly love.

And there was another problem. Benkei brought it up. "You don't much like Yoshinaka, do you?" he asked Yoshitsune one afternoon as they rode back from the training field.

"I don't trust him," answered Yoshitsune scowling. "His eyes are cruel, and he is hungry for power. He's a skilled general, but I pity the captives he will take one day. I think he has no scruples. His swaggering is a bore, and his pompousness would be funny if it were not so savage."

"And yet Yoritomo has made him a general," mused Tadanobu, who had ridden up behind them. "He's really an excellent tactician, and if he's given the chance, he will wage well-conducted campaigns. I agree that he is unpleasant, but that doesn't take away from his military skill."

"That is exactly Yoritomo's view," retorted Yoshitsune. "But to trust a man without honor to do battle is not only base but impractical. Yoshinaka will end by doing battle for his own glory, not for Yoritomo and the Genji."

The powerful *yamabushi* laid his hand on Yoshitsune's sleeve and answered quietly, "Perhaps Yoritomo is more wary of your idealism than of Yoshinaka's treachery."

His men understood Yoshitsune's anger. There were rumors that the leadership of the first attacking Genji army was to be in Yoshinaka's hands.

Yoritomo rarely gave reasons for doing something, and the rumors proved to be right. With no explanation, Yoritomo announced that Yoshinaka was to lead a hand-picked army of one thousand men to the west and engage the Heike in battle. With his usual foresight, Yoritomo could not have chosen a more perfect moment when the time finally arrived. He had counted on everything happening exactly as it did.

There was much confusion throughout Japan during the last six months of 1180. The ministers of the left and right and the entire grand council met to discuss affairs in the capital. Priests chanted sutras from morning to night, arranging for special services and rituals, and their incantations filled the night. The courtiers, rushing helplessly about, were terrified by the thought of an unknown future. Everyone was worried about the new child-Emperor Antoku, who was only two years old. His father, the Emperor Takakura, had been mysteriously ill for months, and was dying.

In addition, in the sixth month of the year, Kiyomori had ordered the entire court to move to a new capital he was building at Fukuhara on the Inland Sea. They were to abandon Kyoto, established as the capital by Emperor Kammu nearly four hundred years before. They were to move all their homes, belongings, and families to a seaside capital which wasn't even finished yet.

Goshirakawa was calm but scornful.

"Kiyomori is acting like a fool," he commented dryly. "I never thought he would go this far."

"It is all so sudden," the minister of the left said, shaking his head in bewilderment.

"Sudden?" The ex-emperor raised a delicate eyebrow. "Not exactly sudden. Kiyomori has always wanted to reopen trade with China as a means of raising money to fill the treasury. For two hundred and fifty years, we have had no official relations with China, and I do not say that one day it would not indeed be a wise thing to open our doors to trade. But to move the entire court now?" Goshirakawa grimaced. "That is his madness."

At Rokuhara, Kiyomori remained firm. He refused to change his decision in any way. The old capital would move to the new. Goshirakawa had been right. There was nothing sudden about it. Kiyomori had been planning it for years. His son Shigemori, the entire court, the monasteries, which did not want to be abandoned by their patrons—everybody tried to halt the thing before it got out of hand.

But Kiyomori stubbornly refused to change his mind, and in the sixth month the entire city was all but completely dismantled and moved south to crowd into the new capital. Goods were floated down the river, entire mansions were torn down and transported, ox-carts crammed the roads, horses, as the easiest means of transportation, were worth a small fortune. And the beautiful city in the sheltered valley was left behind for the cold, foggy, salt winds and acute discomforts ahead. Lamenting and thoroughly miserable, grumbling at every turn, the people endured it for six months.

And during that six months, the thing happened that Kiyomori had tried to prevent, that he had tried not even to think about, because his whole life had been based on its not happening.

War. The Genji army from the east, under the generalship of Yoshinaka, attacked and defeated the Heike forces at the Kiso River.

In the twelfth month, under a gentle winter snow, the court and all the people returned to Kyoto, away from the cold shores and fog back to the inland valley. Their relief and joy was immense. They set about rebuilding their homes and relandscaping their gardens, and began to pick up the threads of their daily lives. The seaside capital at Fukuhara had died in its infancy.

The excitement over the battle at Kiso River soon died down, for the Genji army made no further move. It was even rumored that the battle had not been entirely decisive. And most people in Kyoto blindly refused to admit that in spite of the temporary calm, they were headed for disaster.

But three months later, Kyoto was once again in a state of alarm. The frightened members of the court gathered in small groups, wondering what was to become of them. And the townspeople clamored in the streets. Their talisman of peace, their great protector, the only man capable of standing between them and total disorder was about to abandon them.

At Rokuhara, Kiyomori lay dying.

Calling quickly for his attendants, Goshirakawa set out for the great estate. Peering through the drawn blinds of his carriage as he rode up the tree-lined avenue, he could not help but notice the gloom that hung like a dark cloud over the entire place. At the middle gate the oxen were quickly unhitched and servants pulled the carriage around to the eastern wing.

"How is he?" asked Goshirakawa as Kiyomori's son Shigemori came forward to greet him.

Shigemori's face was thin and haggard. He looked as though he had not slept for days. At Goshirakawa's question, he shook his head.

"I do not think he can last much longer. He is extremely weak." Shigemori paused. "It has all been too much for him."

"He was a great man," said Goshirakawa suddenly. "His saddest misfortune was that he dreamed of peace in a country that is not yet ready for peace."

"And of ships and the sea and his precious harbor, of foreign trade in a country that is almost too bankrupt to have anything to trade at all."

"The Genji will change all that now," said Goshirakawa in a flat voice, "and the change will come swiftly and violently."

"I did not think so years ago, but perhaps the time has come," said Shigemori.

A slight rustle from behind startled them and they turned. A tall, now painfully thin figure was outlined in the pale moonlight of dawn. He had been wandering in the garden outside his beloved red plum hall, and the fragrance of plum blossoms still clung to his sleeves. The edges of his white kimono fluttered as he moved silently toward them.

Kiyomori bent his deep, quiet eyes upon them and said softly, "The time *has* come. Japan needs a stronger arm than mine to lean on now. My failure lay in not seeing that more was needed than simply peace." His breathing grew heavy and he shivered. "And in any case, it would not have mattered. There is an old song. Do you remember it?

> "The sound of the temple bell
> Echoes the impermanence of all things.
> The flowers of the teak tree declare
> That they who flourish must be brought low.
> The proud ones are but for a moment,
> Like an evening dream in springtime.
> The mighty are destroyed at the last;
> They are but as dust before wind.

"What is to come will come. It is all preordained." Kiyomori's eyes were far away. "Yes," he nodded slowly, "the time has come."

The effort of leaving his couch had been too great. His

strength began to fail. On the dais behind his gauze curtains-of-state, Kiyomori lay still.

At Kamakura, Yoshitsune stormed furiously into Yoritomo's apartments. Contrary to custom, he had even forgotten to remove his long sword before entering the presence of the chieftain of the Genji. Yoritomo had been engaged in serious discussion with two of his advisors, and he glanced up coldly at this unannounced and unwelcome interruption.

"Do manage to learn to control yourself," said Yoritomo, staring at the flushed and angry face of his younger brother. "This is really too much. Such passion is neither becoming nor useful."

Even angrier now because of Yoritomo's insulting lecture in front of the others and because of the coldness with which he was received, Yoshitsune hurled his words across the room.

"He is dead! Kiyomori is dead. Without ever knowing the sting of our revenge for father's death. So be it. Our victory will be revenge enough. But to keep me here!" Yoshitsune's voice trembled with rage. "To keep me here and send in my stead that vicious cutthroat Yoshinaka. Granted he won the battle at Kiso River. It was well done, but I could have done the same. But now he is marching on the capital, and I shudder to think of the dishonor he will bring to the name of Genji. He will not bring justice and order to Kyoto, he will plunder and destroy it. They will curse us as barbarians!"

"And you want them to welcome us as saviors," mocked Yoritomo. He rose and faced his brother. "Now listen to me. I shall explain this because I owe it to you as my brother. Any other man I would dismiss without a word. I have great regard both for your honorable scruples and for your military skills. I shall tell you frankly that I think you are going to be the greatest general I shall ever have by my side. And that is precisely why I am not going to be fool enough to let you waste your efforts now. The most crucial times are yet to come. Yoshinaka is clever and ruthless enough to clear the way, but he is by no means capable of destroying the Heike. When that time comes, I shall leave the matter in your hands. Do I make myself clear?"

"Perfectly." Yoshitsune turned on his heel and left the room.

As Yoshitsune talked of all this later with his chosen band, Tsugunobu said quietly, "I think there is another reason—one that maybe he doesn't even realize himself. I think he is jealous of you."

"Of me?" Yoshitsune was genuinely surprised. "But why of me?"

"He sees in you greatness and strength and courage, and he cannot help but notice the loyalty you inspire among the men you lead."

"But I have no wish to take Yoritomo's place," said Yoshitsune. "It is his right and privilege to be chief of our clan, not only because he is Yoshitomo's eldest son, but because he, better than anyone else, has the wisdom and capacity to rule Japan."

"He knows that. And he also thinks you are far too impulsive, too ruled by passion to survive very long. But it is just this passion, the way you are able to feel, to inspire feeling in others, that he does not understand and therefore envies."

Yoshinaka marched on the capital with all the barbarity of his ferocious nature. Terrorized, the Heike fled before him, taking the child-Emperor Antoku with them. In the dead of night, they wrapped him and his baby Fujiwara consort in garments of brown and smuggled them out of the palace. The little emperor was Kiyomori's grandson, and they felt his fate would be terrible if he fell into the hands of the Genji. With Antoku went his grandmother, the widow of Kiyomori. The Heike, with their emperor, retreated as fast as possible to the southern islands of Shikoku and Kyushu where their fleet was waiting.

And Yoshinaka lorded over the capital, proclaiming himself Shogun, commander-in-chief. His soldiers roamed loose, ravaging and plundering as they chose, until the city was completely subdued.

Goshirakawa, in his Cloister Palace, waited for Yoritomo's next move, patient, and utterly confident. The willow, bending with the wind, is never destroyed.

# The Way of Bow and Horse

The Heike fled to the south with the emperor, taking with them also the three sacred imperial treasures, the jewel, the sword, and the mirror. Here they tried to establish some sort of order in their lives. They built a palace of rough timber on the shore for their emperor, and the courtiers spent their days in thatched fishermen's huts listening to the clamor of the waves and the cries of the wild geese. Their great hope lay in Kiyomori's sons, Munemori, who was now commander-in-chief; and Tomomori, his first general. Shigemori, in his grief, had not survived his father's death.

In the capital, Yoshinaka's power grew daily. He had gained the support of the mighty *yamabushi* of Mount Hiei, and since the priests had had enough of the arrogant Heike, they were ready to welcome the Genji. Goshirakawa found the rough swaggering of the Genji soldiers through his capital distasteful, but he knew better than to say so. He knew that Yoritomo would not permit it to go on much longer. And so he bided his time.

The time came in 1184.

"Bring me his head!" The quiet, terrible voice of Yoritomo resounded through the great hall at Kamakura.

Yoshitsune strode up to the dais, where his brother put a heavy paper in his fist. The large seal of the retired Emperor Goshirakawa was affixed to the message.

"So," breathed Yoshitsune. "Yoshinaka thinks he can make and unmake emperors in the capital." His face darkened in a burst of fury. "He has damaged the capital, insulted the court, enraged the monks, made a mockery of our name. And now this! The people clamor for the return of their emperor, and he pacifies them by creating a new emperor, Go-Toba. How dare he!"

Yoshitsune paused to regain control of his temper. He and Yoritomo exchanged a long look.

"Now?" asked Yoshitsune quietly.

Yoritomo nodded. "Now. I want the sacred jewel, the sword, and the mirror, taken by the Heike, returned to the imperial court, Antoku replaced on the throne—and the Heike destroyed." Yoritomo paused.

"And I want Yoshinaka's head. You will take Noriyori, our half-brother, to share the command and leave within the week," thundered Yoritomo.

Five hundred strong, the hand-picked army of the Genji followed Yoshitsune out of Kamakura to the west. The mounted warriors were the mightiest archers, the boldest horsemen, the most brilliant swordsmen of the land. They were followed by expertly trained, lightly armored foot soldiers, carrying halberds and grapnels. It was the army that Yoshitsune himself had trained. Although more men had been offered to him, he wanted no others. This was his command, and they were tuned to each other and to their leader like the strings of a fine instrument.

He rode before them, leading them on. His general's armor

was an ancestral treasure of the Genji clan. The powdered gold lacquer plates were laced with braided silver cord; the skirts and shoulder pieces were wide and full; and the breastplate was covered with exquisite brocade of purple and gold. The under-robe, bloused and fastened below the knees and at the wrists, was of white damask traced in lavender, and the billowing mantle, which hung from his shoulders, white silk. His helmet was adorned with gilded horns, and his padded gloves and the *tabi* on his feet were of cloth of gold. On his back were the bow, which stood taller than a man, and a quiver of arrows, fifteen handbreadths in length, tipped with eagle feathers. At his waist was an ancient and precious sword, four and a half feet long, with a carved handle and scabbard, and a small, jeweled dagger.

"He is like the sun," whispered the men. And they followed him with joy.

The mighty host rode onward, over the mountains, through the rivers, across the plains.

And one night, from a vantage point near Kyoto, their bonfires leaped into a roaring blaze. It was the Hour of the Boar, not yet midnight, and the fires were easily seen. Outriders rode into the city. And several retainers burst into the rooms at the palace, where Yoshinaka now lived, in an agony of terror for their master.

"They have come! To the south of the city, near Uji. Yoritomo's army has arrived."

Yoshinaka paused in the middle of a drunken brawl. He knew why the army had come, and he grew pale as the waning moon.

And as the sun rose the following morning, at the Hour of the Tiger, the two armies faced each other across the Uji River. The roaring of distant rapids echoed the hollow boom of the war drums.

Yoshitsune and Noriyori stared critically at their opponents. "They are several hundred stronger than we," commented Noriyori.

"Stronger? Just that many more to get in each other's way," replied Yoshitsune briefly.

"Our men will be ready to start in an hour or so."

Yoshitsune stared at him. "They are ready now."

And he turned to the captain of the advance archers. "Everybody mounted and in position in ten minutes. When you see me draw my bow, that is the signal to begin. See that the foot soldiers are kept to the rear and out of the way of the horses until I call for them."

Yoshitsune led his army to the river's edge; and the men, inspired by his bold courage, rushed to follow him. Drawing a shaft with a humming-bulb tip, the traditional beginning of a battle, Yoshitsune sent it whistling in a wide arc across the river. A rain of arrows flew from both sides until the air was blackened with the moving shafts. The practiced skill of Yoshitsune's archers began to take effect. Drawing bowstring after bowstring, calmly and without letup, they kept a barrage of arrows crossing the river until Yoshinaka's army began to fall back.

As they drew back from the river's edge, Yoshitsune snapped his iron-ribbed fan as the signal for the left phalanx to cross the river. Crouching low over their horses so as not to be caught in the back by the arrows that continued to cover their crossing, they urged their mounts into the river. They fought the swelling currents of the Uji River and managed to reach the far bank. Immediately, they attacked the enemy archers to stop their fire long enough for the rest of the Genji army to cross the river, to begin hand-to-hand combat on the field beyond.

The swiftness of such maneuvering staggered Yoshinaka's army. Many of them fled from the field in terror. Yoshitsune's men grappled furiously with those remaining, who still outnumbered them. In one place, a single warrior, cut off from his fellows, pulled off his green mantle and threw it deftly over the heads of the three men who were attacking him. Then he sped around them and galloped off in the direction of Yoshinaka, who was surrounded by his bodyguard. The bodyguard was so busy fending the warrior off, that they did not notice another group of warriors, who having seen what was going on, took advantage of the moment to come around from the rear. The warrior of the green mantle was killed instantly, but the others from behind, led by Tadanobu, managed to destroy most of the bodyguard. Yoshinaka himself got away.

In another place the advance archers managed to push through and get far enough behind the enemy's rear to be able to draw their bows from there. The confusion caused by being shot at from behind and attacked by sword and halberd from the other three sides made any unified effort in Yoshinaka's army all but impossible.

The fighting closed in until there was almost a solid mass of glittering armor and swords. Helmets were smashed, breastplates were cut in half as though they were paper. The air resounded with the crash of steel on steel, mingled with hoarse cries and the screams of frightened horses. By twos and threes warriors grappled with each other and fell to the ground, reaching for their daggers. Some took heads, others were beheaded. Dust rose into the sky, and the earth was spattered with blood and sweat. Those who managed to remain on their horses wheeled in and out of the struggling mass, attacking again and again, coming at one another in individual combat with the skill of mighty warriors.

The mightiest and most feared sword of all was Yoshitsune's. Able to loose his pent up rage at last, he slashed and cut down all before him. The Genji banner glimmered in the morning sun, and Yoshitsune wielded his sword proudly, fiercely, victoriously. He was everywhere at once, his strength flowed into the hearts of his men, and as he fought he cried words of encouragement to them.

Plunging his sword into the last of his immediate attackers, Yoshitsune looked around for Yoshinaka.

"Look at that," he yelled to Benkei, who had risked his life time and again to stay at his master's side.

The two tore off in a gallop to the other end of the field. Yoshitsune waved his war fan, crying out, "Yoshinaka, come back. Do not bring disgrace to the name of Genji by showing your back to an enemy. Yoshinaka!"

Yoshinaka turned his horse for a second. The dappled gray steed reared its forelegs into the air and plunged away across the battlefield. Urging on Black Lacquer, whose speed was unequaled, Yoshitsune raced after the departing Yoshinaka. Overtaking him at last, he challenged his cousin in combat.

"Why should we fight?" Yoshinaka panted. "There is no reason for us to shed each other's blood."

Yoshitsune glared at him angrily. "You have dishonored the name of Genji. Though you are my cousin, you are everything

I despise—cowardly, cruel, without personal honor. And you have betrayed Yoritomo who sent you here in good faith. You have had repeated warnings, but still you went on plundering the capital, dishonoring the imperial crown. Yoritomo has sentenced you to death, and you ought to be grateful to die on the battle-field instead of being hung like a thief." As he spoke, Yoshitsune drew his sword, and raising it high above his head, called on Yoshinaka to defend himself.

Yoshinaka drew his sword and they fought, exchanging thrust for thrust and blow for blow while Benkei fended off all who would interfere. The Hour of the Dragon had just begun when Yoshitsune brought his sword arm down with all his might, and in an instant Yoshinaka was dead. According to tradition, Yoshitsune cut off Yoshinaka's head and wrapped it in a piece of silk. Then he called for a special head box. He entrusted the head box to several retainers, ordering them to bring it to Yoritomo in token of victory.

With Yoshinaka's death, the battle was over. Yoshitsune returned with his army to the camp beyond the Uji River. To his chief officers he gave orders that those of Yoshinaka's army who survived and had not fled were to be brought to him.

"They are ready, my lord, and waiting for your inspection."

Yoshitsune strode out of his tent and examined the remnants of Yoshinaka's forces. His own army had suffered fewer than fifty losses, and all but a few of the wounded were out of serious danger. But of Yoshinaka's army there remained fewer than three hundred men, the others killed or vanished. Among them were many brave warriors whom Yoshitsune knew by sight or by reputation and who were both relieved and glad to be under Yoshitsune's command instead of that of his cousin. These men Yoshitsune accepted into his own ranks. A few warriors he knew to be scoundrels without honor; these were put to death as traitors. Among the foot soldiers, he weeded out the rabble and assigned the rest as retainers to his men. Altogether, two hundred and fifty were added to his ranks; they were now seven hundred strong.

As they sat in the tent later that evening eating a light supper of dried fish, pickles, and rice, and passing around the jar of hot sake, the men spoke of the day's events, each recounting the part of the battle he had seen and fought.

Tadanobu, who was Yoshitsune's most expert officer, cool, methodical, and completely fearless, spoke first.

"My compliments, my lord," he said, raising his cup of rice wine to Yoshitsune. "Your timing today was the most perfect I have ever been privileged to see."

"The men responded well," replied Yoshitsune, but his eyes shone with pleasure at the admiration of his men.

"You trained them," said Kijiro, whose marksmanship as leader of the advance archers that day had been superb.

"And you, Tsugunobu," scolded Yoshitsune in mock crossness, but with a note of real concern in his voice, "the next time you throw yourself in front of me like that and take an arrow in your arm that was meant for mine, I shall have you horsewhipped."

Tsugunobu smiled one of his rare smiles and said nothing, merely lifting his cup in toast to his general.

"And Benkei," continued Yoshitsune in the same tone of voice, "you are not to keep interfering with me on the field."

Benkei had spent the entire battle fending off with his powerful sword all who approached his chieftain.

"Then stop looking for trouble," growled Benkei. "You are not a common soldier to plunge right into the middle of everything."

"He's right," agreed Kisanta. "There are still thousands more Heike than Genji, and one day soon we shall have to face them. Yoritomo has promised to send another thousand men, but the odds are still greatly against us. The one difference is that this Genji army has you. It is your spirit that makes us strong."

Proudly he added, "One day you shall be remembered as the greatest warlord in Japanese history."

The others nodded in complete agreement.

Yoshitsune, moved to tears by such devotion, could not speak. One by one they bowed deeply and left the tent to see to their horses and the men.

As Yoshitsune lay staring up at the frosty winter sky late that night, Benkei crept to his side.

"You must try to sleep. You haven't closed your eyes tonight."

"It's no use. I'm in no mood for sleep. You know, Benkei, it's strange. Death filled the morning, and men rose in battle to kill one another for the honor of their gods and their ancestors. And tonight the winds push the clouds across the sky and never note the deeds of men at all."

Benkei was silent for a moment. Then he said softly, "I know something else that bothers you."

Propping himself on his arm, Yoshitsune nodded. "Yes. I am worried about Kyo-no-Kimi."

"She is protected, both as the daughter of a Genji ally and as lady-in-waiting to the ex-empress. Shall we enter the capital tomorrow? Then you can see her. The Heike took the little emperor with them, and of course Kiyomori's family left, but most of the court is still safely in Kyoto."

Yoshitsune smiled. "At least now I have more to offer her than I did as a penniless young outlaw." A worried frown followed the smile. "I wonder though if she remembers me. I haven't forgotten her for a moment, but for her perhaps eight and a half years is too long a time. So much happens at court, and so quickly. By now she may even be married."

"You will soon find out," said Benkei.

"Perhaps not so soon. It depends."

"Aren't we marching to Kyoto tomorrow?" Benkei asked.

Yoshitsune shook his head. "Tomorrow we will attack the Heike. I got word a few hours ago that they are encamped at

Ichi-no-Tani. Now, while they are overconfident and our men are strong with victory, is the time to attack."

Several weeks before, the Heike had left the southern islands and crossed their fleet over to the mainland. Encouraged that the Genji were fighting each other, they confidently set up camp at Ichi-no-Tani, on a strip of seacoast that was nearly impossible to get to. There was the sea in front of them, and a beach road—but these were extremely well defended. Close behind them rose an almost sheer wall of high, steep cliffs. Here the Heike remained, amassing their forces. They were waiting, hoping against hope that the Genji would destroy themselves.

"You will have trouble persuading Noriyori to agree to an attack," commented Benkei.

Yoshitsune laughed. "I have no intention of consulting Noriyori. He is so cautious that I'm not at all sure he isn't just plain lazy. I know Yoritomo had Noriyori share my command as a check to my impulsiveness. But since I know far more about these matters than Noriyori does, I am prepared to take full responsibility for what happens. If Yoritomo is displeased, I cannot help it. The reason we are here is to defeat the Heike and to restore order in the capital. I see no point in dragging it out. I'm going to take every advantage of our position at the moment. We shall attack the Heike tomorrow."

With one glance at the set mouth and shining eyes of his master, Benkei knew better than to attempt to argue with him. So he hid his misgivings and pulled a flute from the small brocade bag attached to his sash. He played far into the night, and finally soothed Yoshitsune into a deep sleep.

# Ichi-no-Tani

"We shall follow the Yodo River southwest to Naniwa on the Inland Sea. Then we travel west along the coast until we reach Ichi-no-Tani."

Yoshitsune, using the tip of his war fan, traced the route on a large map spread on the ground before him. The officers gathered around him and watched. "We shall travel light and very fast. Needless to say, we shall be greatly outnumbered. The Heike army is several thousand strong, and we are less than a thousand. And yet we have the greater advantage. Surprise. They won't expect us so soon. What is more, our men are far better trained, and the Heike are soft. If we attack quickly enough, with one great thrust, we can cause enough confusion to push them into the sea to their ships. The sea is their only means of retreat." Yoshitsune glanced around, smiling. "And if you all pray for bad weather, they won't be able to move their ships in close enough to shoot from them."

"You forget something," said Noriyori stubbornly. His disapproval of Yoshitsune's plan was clear. But though his rank was equal to Yoshitsune's, he found that the army was Yoshitsune's, not his, to command.

117

"Please speak," said Yoshitsune graciously. As a member of his family, Yoshitsune did not want Noriyori to lose face.

The center of attention momentarily, Noriyori cleared his throat.

"It is all very well to point out the disadvantages of their secure position. But may I also remind you that their position *is* secure. I don't see how we can even get to them, much less attack."

"Well spoken," Yoshitsune replied. "But I don't think we can decide on the approach until we get there. And since this is too excellent an opportunity to lose, I am sure we will find a way."

"And you plan to move the entire army without even a final plan?" Noriyori was clearly amazed.

"I do," replied Yoshitsune quietly. "We can't afford to delay the attack. If the Heike decide to march north in full numbers it will be nearly impossible to defeat them."

There was nothing more to say. By noon the army was on the move, marching along the banks of the Yodo River. They camped that night near Eguchi, a few miles north of Naniwa, and the following night reached the cliffs of Ichi-no-Tani. Showing the perfect discipline of which the Genji army was capable, they pitched camp without a sound, almost directly above the heads of the enemy. The smallest noise would carry far out to sea, and should the Heike hear them, the battle would be lost before it was begun.

With Tadanobu and the captain of the advance archers by his side, together with three of his best officers, Yoshitsune crept to the edge of the cliffs and stared down.

"It is too dark to study the face of the cliffs," he whispered.

A heavy fog made it impossible to see more than a few feet; they had no means of figuring out a way down.

"There is a village just up that road." Yoshitsune pointed. "Come."

Stealthily they crept back, careful not to unloose any stones to roll down and betray their presence.

"What do you think?" asked Tadanobu.

"Clearly the only way to take them by surprise is to go straight down those cliffs and attack them from behind. The road along the beach is too open and is well defended."

Even Tadanobu gasped. "Down those cliffs? But that would be sheer suicide."

"That is what I mean to find out." Yoshitsune looked ahead. "There is the village. We shall need a guide. Someone who knows these hills and cliffs. A boy who will not ask too many questions and who will be happy to earn a reward for his help." Yoshitsune beckoned to one of his retainers. "It is late now. No one will be about. Stay here at the edge of the village until dawn and choose a guide for us. Be very quiet and do not draw any attention to yourself."

"I understand," said the retainer, bowing. "I shall return to camp with a guide by the Hour of the Tiger."

Toward midnight, a cold, dank wind blew in from the sea. A heavy storm was brewing across the waters, driving the swollen tide. Breakers heaved their spray high into the blackness of the night and crashed against the rocks. For an instant, the moon stared brilliantly through an opening in the clouds before they rammed together again. The torrents were blinding at first and then, with the passage of the night, lessened to a steady, gentle downpour.

The army of the Genji, used to such hardships, took the storm in stride. But in the Heike camp below, the storm created havoc. Huddled inside their fisherman's huts, the smoke of driftwood in their noses, the Heike sat and dreamed of their curtained rooms at home. Their faces, long without court make-up, were haggard and worn. Soaked to the skin, they thought not of war, but of beautiful court ladies with white skin, delicately blackened teeth, and dark hair that flowed to the floor.

Munemori sat in his hut. "We cannot remain here much longer." He sighed. "We shall either have to return to our ships . . ."

"Or march on the capital," Tomomori said, completing his brother's sentence.

Just before dawn, two figures appeared at the opening of Yoshitsune's tent. Yoshitsune gave them dry clothing and a light breakfast before questioning them, and the two were most grateful.

"The boy was on his way from the village with his bow and arrow," explained the retainer, wiping his mouth with his sleeve. "He seemed a likely guide, and when I spoke to him, he agreed to come. He says he wants nothing in return for serving you."

The boy interrupted darkly. "The Heike killed my father."

"I understand," said Yoshitsune. "They killed my father, too. Instead of payment, then, please honor me by accepting this." He presented the boy with his own warm hunting cloak.

Openmouthed at such kindly and respectful treatment, the boy was speechless.

Yoshitsune explained matters to him quickly.

Half an hour later, as the sun lightened a still heavy sky, Yoshitsune led his army to the edge of the cliffs. He noted with satisfaction that the sea was still rough. Turning in his saddle, he beckoned to Noriyori and his officers.

He said to Noriyori, "I shall need to depend on you a great deal."

Noriyori looked doubtful but pleased.

Yoshitsune continued. "I shall ask a number of men to volunteer to follow me down the face of this cliff."

Noriyori gasped. "You cannot do that. It would be suicide. Look at that drop."

The boy came forward. "Excuse me," he said awkwardly. "But this honorable gentleman is right. Only a deer can go down those cliffs."

Yoshitsune paused for a moment. "Where a deer can go, so can a horse," he said firmly. "And while we surprise them from behind, Noriyori, you will lead the bulk of the army down the beach road. It is well defended now, but our attack from the rear will frighten them. It will draw their attention while you break through on the beach. We shall have them in a trap."

Providing the plan succeeded, its logic was perfect. Yoshitsune's tactical genius was indeed unsurpassed. If he managed to get his horsemen down the cliffs, there could be no doubt of the outcome of the battle.

"Very well," agreed Noriyori, defeated by Yoshitsune's courage. "What shall be the signal for me to attack?"

Yoshitsune grinned. "The yowling of the Heike," was his answer.

Then, turning to his mounted warriors, he said, "Who among you wishes to follow me down the face of these cliffs? I need not tell you that the descent will be dangerous, but when it is done, the Heike will be ours."

Without hesitation every hand went up, and Yoshitsune smiled his pleasure. He would ask nothing of them he would not ask of himself, but it pleased him to see them seek danger so eagerly. He rode among them and carefully chose thirty of the best horsemen. The rest of the army prepared to follow Noriyori down the beach road.

With the Sato brothers, the Yoshioka brothers, Benkei, and twenty-five others, Yoshitsune waited at the top of the cliffs. He waited until an outrider returned to inform him that Noriyori had reached the far end of the beach road several miles down the coast. He waited another fifteen minutes until Noriyori should have made some progress down the beach. And then, with a swift prayer to Hachiman, the god of war, he gave the signal for his small band to start.

Riding before his men, with the village boy to guide them down the treacherous ridges, Yoshitsune urged Black Lacquer

on. Under the calm hand of his master, the horse moved fear-
lessly. The slope was so steep that the feet of the warrior behind
were on a level with the helmet of the warrior in front. Slowly,
they picked their way, muscles tensed to hold their balance,
straining to guide the feet of the horses to prevent them from
breaking a leg. Silently they rode, one by one, down and farther
down the cliffs. A hundred yards from the bottom, the way
became nothing but great, mossy boulders, and Yoshitsune
sensed that the men and horses were terrified. Turning in his
stirrups to reassure them, he saw Tadanobu suddenly ride forward, the spirit of the Tengu shining in his face, yelling as he
came.

"Where I come from we would make of this a race course, or
ride down it any day to fell a deer!"

Down he went by Yoshitsune's side, and the rest came after
him with renewed courage. Swords glittering in their upraised
hands, they crashed down on the enemy.

The Heike were taken completely by surprise. In horror and
confusion, they tumbled out of their huts into the hands of the
waiting Genji. Their first yells were echoed a mile down the
beach road by the rest of the Heike, who had just been attacked
by Noriyori. Cutting, slashing, and swinging in all directions,
the Genji soon made complete havoc of the Heike camp. It was
one of the fastest and fiercest battles ever fought. Yoshitsune
flashed like lightning among his soldiers, leading attacks, reform-
ing their groups, heading off the fleeing Heike. He kept confusion at its height, knowing that the slightest letup would
provide the Heike, who outnumbered his own army, with the
chance to do considerable damage. It was not long before
Yoshitsune had accomplished what he wished.

Some of the Heike remained on the beach to fight and be
killed, and nearly two thousand lost their lives that day at
Ichi-no-Tani. Most of them, however, fled to their ships anchored
just off the shore, many praying the death prayer as they went.

"O Amida Nyorai who sheddest the light of Thy Presence through the ten quarters of the world, gather into Thy Radiant Heaven all who call upon Thy Name!"

And they plunged into the waves.

A Genji captain watched a single Heike horseman fleeing to one of the ships and cried out, "You ought to be ashamed to show your back to an enemy!"

The Heike warrior wheeled his horse around and returned to the beach. Slashing his armor and hurling him to the ground, the Genji captain, Kumagai Naozane, tore off his opponent's helmet and saw the youthful face. The boy could not have been more than sixteen or seventeen, with beautiful features and the delicately powdered face and blackened teeth of a courtier. The Heike youth reminded Kumagai of his own son; he did not have the heart to take the boy's life. But just then a group of Genji horsemen rode up, and Kumagai knew if he did not kill the young Heike, they would.

I shall have to suffer the burden of this boy's life, he thought bitterly. What utter madness these horrible wars are. And then aloud he said, "What is your name? Who are you?"

"I am Atsumori, youngest son of Tsunemori and nephew to Kiyomori. Take my head, for it will bring you honor on your side."

"It will neither bring us victory nor cause our defeat should you die," whispered Kumagai miserably. "And yet if I don't kill you, those warriors will. You cannot escape. So if it is to be, let it be by my hand, and I will see that you are buried with the honor of your rank."

"For that I thank you," answered Atsumori, and he bared his neck.

And when Kumagai laid him gently down, he found among his clothing a flute in a brocade bag. He remembered the music he had heard floating up from the beach that morning.

"So it was Atsumori who played so beautifully before battle.

How gentle he must have been." Kumagai knew he would remember the youth all his days. Of such small incidents, he thought, are large battles made.

Kajiwara, one of Yoshitsune's best generals, came riding up triumphantly. "It is over, my lord. The day is ours."

Yoshitsune stared out toward the ships. "Today we have won. But thousands of Heike have escaped, and we have not yet gotten back either the emperor or the imperial regalia. There is still much to be done."

"I am sure it will all be managed in due time," replied Kajiwara, in a voice that was a mixture of cunning politeness and sarcasm.

Yoshitsune eyed the burly general, who had changed over from the Heike to the Genji side. Yoshitsune saw that this surly warrior had only his own interests at heart, and disliked him. His answer was curt.

"You will see that the wounded are attended to and that the men get some rest. We march to the capital in the morning."

Kajiwara saluted him and rode off.

"I don't trust him," growled Benkei. "Why not let me rid you of him once and for all?"

Yoshitsune glanced with amusement at the towering figure of his follower.

"You fuss over me like an old fox over its young."

"Well, you refuse to look after your own welfare. How long shall we remain in Kyoto?" asked Benkei as the Sato and Yoshioka brothers joined them.

"Not long enough for the men to grow soft. But I must reassure the court—and particularly Goshirakawa—that we are not all like Yoshinaka, and that they would do well to lend us whatever support they can."

Yoshitsune paused, worried. "I must also persuade him to lend us ships immediately. We don't have time to wait until Yoritomo's fleet arrives. We must attack the Heike fleet before they have time to recover."

Tadanobu nodded in approval.

Kijiro laughed. "Tadanobu worries about wasting too much time in pleasure. I for one shall enjoy the change. It's a long time that we've been away, and I am sure there are several ladies in the gay quarters who have missed me terribly. I remember one in particular . . ."

"All right, all right," Benkei interrupted. "Spare us the details."

Kijiro began to examine his face, mirrored in a circle of polished bronze.

"You are still beautiful," said Kisanta, sighing mockingly.

Laughing, they all went to bed.

It was a happy and victorious army that reached Kyoto the following day. The white banner of the Genji fluttered from poles, and newly polished armor glittered in the sunlight. The war horses pranced and the musicians played. It was near sunset as the army passed through the great southern pillars of the Rashomon Gate, and as Yoshitsune led his victorious army through, he could not help remembering the way in which he had left Kyoto nearly nine years before. From the merry sparkle in the eyes of his five most devoted followers, he knew they remembered, too.

# At Court

When Goshirakawa had heard that Yoshitsune was on his way to the capital, he had arranged for a great banquet to be held. He knew perfectly well that the Genji preferred strict warrior ways. But Goshirakawa had no intention of appearing to slight them. He had also heard that Yoshitsune was not quite so against gracious pleasures as his brother Yoritomo. Dances and a concert and later a poetry contest were to be held, and on the following day, archery competitions and horse races to please the warriors.

When Yoshitsune received the invitation just after his arrival in Kyoto, he ordered court robes for himself.

Noriyori did not approve. "It is bad enough that you are going. But to go in court robes instead of a warrior's armor—that is too much. We must teach this Goshirakawa and his court a lesson."

Yoshitsune raised an eyebrow. "What lesson?"

"That it is we, not they, who are now in charge. And that we will not put up with any more extravagance. Whatever you do, I am going in armor."

"You have a great deal to learn, Noriyori," replied Yoshitsune with contempt. "Don't think because we have won a battle that we have beaten the Heike. We need Goshirakawa's support, and

127

if we do not offend him, he seems quite willing to give it."

"But he has no choice," said Noriyori angrily.

"Not in the long run, no," answered Yoshitsune quietly. "One day Yoritomo will have complete power in his hands. But in the meantime, Goshirakawa could make trouble if he wished."

"How?" asked Noriyori in disbelief.

"He has wealth and ships and allies. I would prefer them on our side. He could also stir the monks against us, for they are still angry at the way Yoshinaka treated them. And I want peace here in the capital. We have no time for squabbling; we must attack the Heike again before they recover. And one more thing. I think that with a little tact and another victory or two, we could persuade some of the families that have still not taken sides to join us." Yoshitsune stared hard at Noriyori. "Is all this clear?"

Noriyori's face was stony. "It seems to me you have taken a great deal upon yourself. We shall see what Yoritomo has to say about all this."

And he strode from the room.

On the day of the festival a soft wind blew in from the Eastern Hills, and the morning was bright and clear. The sun shone softly on the court lawns and gardens, and rays of sunlight pierced the outer shutters of palace apartments. Behind them, the ladies and gentlemen of the court were busily dressing for the festivities. When they appeared with their pages along the corridors and verandas overlooking the Southern Court, the effect was indeed splendid. The little heir apparent to the throne, Go-Toba, was led in among the company in his royal yellow silken robes. He was attended by ten boy outriders, their hair looped at the sides and tied with purple ribbons. The grand minister appeared in a moss green cloak, followed by a dozen pages dressed in white tunics. The ex-Empress Tokuko, who was still fashionable at court, sat behind gauze curtains with her ladies.

Goshirakawa, followed by his entire retinue, arrived by midafternoon with the greatest possible elegance and grace, handsomely robed in a purple cloak and brocaded trousers.

The large assembly of princes and nobles and court ladies wondered aloud about Yoshitsune. Some expected an uncouth barbarian, others a grim-faced warrior. When, half an hour later, Yoshitsune appeared, there were gasps and murmurs of surprise. They had expected anything but what they saw. The poise, elegance, and nobility of the figure who stood before them astounded them as the worst display of barbarism could not have done. They had simply never imagined that anybody brought up outside the court could be civilized.

A brilliant crimson cloak hung gracefully from his shoulders. Beneath the cloak he wore a close-fitting robe of lavender silk in the latest fashion and long white trousers woven with silver threads. In the entire court, his charm, grace, and beauty were unrivaled; and even Goshirakawa found himself moved by the handsome dignity of the young man. The graciousness with which he performed his obeisance before the ex-emperor won for Yoshitsune a greater acclaim than any battle could have accomplished.

With elaborate ceremony, Goshirakawa welcomed Yoshitsune of the Genji to the place of honor. The Sato brothers, the Yoshioka brothers, and Benkei accompanied him.

"Shall we begin the entertainment or await the arrival of Noriyori?" asked Goshirakawa. "I would not want you to be bored, nor should I wish to insult your half-brother. Or perhaps he is not coming?"

Goshirakawa's pleasantries were suddenly interrupted by the arrival of Noriyori. In full armor, his sword glittering at his side, Noriyori strode across the court lawn attended by a fully armed bodyguard. It was an insult, Yoshitsune realized, that could not possibly have been misunderstood. Noriyori paused before Goshirakawa and bowed shortly.

After an abrupt greeting, he said, "I am not used to court

ceremony as you are. You will forgive me if I do not remain. It would merely make both of us uncomfortable."

He left immediately. Goshirakawa noted right away, from the narrow glance exchanged by the brothers, the rivalry and intense dislike that existed between them. He wondered whether Yoritomo would use this to his own purpose or choose simply to ignore it.

Yoshitsune had honored the imperial throne, and wisely so. While the throne had no military force, it had the power which comes of being sacred. It was stupid, as well as sacrilegious, to affront it. It was for Yoshitsune's honor to the throne, as well as his greater strength and intelligence, that Goshirakawa chose to continue the banquet in Yoshitsune's honor instead of calling it off to please Noriyori. Clapping his hands, the ex-emperor called for the festivities to begin.

After the first dances, presents were given to the whole court. Among other things, Yoshitsune received a gold-studded saddle from Goshirakawa.

It was then that nameless hour, neither day nor yet night. The fragrance of fruit blossoms and the harmonies of string and flute filled the air. One after the other, the courtiers performed on their musical instruments, and all were astonished at how beautifully Yoshitsune played his flute.

The banquet lasted until dawn, and it was not until the morning birds interrupted the concert that the guests made ready to leave.

As he wandered back along the pavilions to the outer court where his carriage was waiting, Yoshitsune was still not ready for sleep. Throughout the whole evening, his gaze had turned toward the gaily colored hangings behind which he knew the ex-empress sat with her ladies. It tortured him to think that Kyo-no-Kimi was there, only a few feet away from him, and that court manners forbade him to speak to her.

"Yes, she was there," said Benkei. A grin lit up the rough,

good-natured face. "I asked. But surely you don't plan to visit her now!" When he saw from the stubborn set of his master's jaw that he had guessed right, Benkei's voice grew alarmed. "My lord, you can't go barging into ladies' rooms at this hour, particularly those of the ex-empress's ladies. Wait until evening, until I can arrange something."

As much as he wanted to see Kyo-no-Kimi, Yoshitsune realized that Benkei was right. Returning to his apartments in the Cloister Palace, where Goshirakawa had insisted he stay until more permanent quarters could be arranged, Yoshitsune slept fitfully for a few hours. But by early afternoon he was up again, choosing gifts for Kyo-no-Kimi and composing a poem to go with them.

This pleasant pastime was constantly interrupted by callers and messengers from the court nobles who wished to pay their respects. Senior advisors, chamberlains, members of the grand council, courtiers of the first to the fifth rank, and even the minister of the right sent elaborate messages of welcome. His rooms were filled with pages and attendants who had accompanied the royal visitors, and there was much excitement.

By early evening, Yoshitsune was finally able to escape. Accompanied by Benkei and several outriders, he made his way to the southern end of the Kokiden, the Empress's Palace, where ex-Empress Tokuko still lived. He had heard that Kyo-no-Kimi was her favorite companion. It would not be easy to see her alone, but he had bribed one of the palace maids and hoped for the best.

The maid came quickly and led Yoshitsune down an outer corridor and across a little bridge, which connected to another building. Pausing in front of a room with latticed windows, she motioned Yoshitsune to enter. Here he waited for what seemed like a very long time.

Suddenly he heard a rustle, and his heart leaped. She did not let him see her right away, but remained behind a screen. This hurt him. But then he heard the soft plucking of a lute, and tears filled his eyes. She was playing the same song she had played that lovely moonlit evening at Uji. That was her way of welcoming him, her way of telling him that nothing had changed. Yoshitsune was so happy he could barely breathe. So much changed so quickly in this world. Had he found at last the thing in which he could trust and believe?

Wishing to return her thoughts in the same manner, he drew the fan of hinoki wood from his sleeve and pushed it under the silken hangings. The music stopped suddenly, and he heard a faint gasp as she recognized the fan.

Had he really carried it all that time? Kyo-no-Kimi hardly dared to believe in such a miracle.

Yoshitsune could wait no longer to see her. He could no longer bear to be so near her and yet not see her. Quickly he pushed the hangings aside. She was more beautiful than he remembered. The rising flush in her cheeks made the pale face even lovelier. Softly he caressed the shining black hair and looked long and deeply into the dark sweetness of her eyes. She uttered a faint cry as his arms closed strongly about her, and burying her face against his neck, she clung to him for a long time.

"Come," said Yoshitsune gently. "Have your gentlewomen dress you warmly and pack a few things. We must hurry now."

Kyo-no-Kimi's eyes widened in alarm.

Yoshitsune's voice was almost rough as he grasped her fragile shoulders, "We can't go on meeting like this. It may be very well for the gentlemen at court to prowl around at night visiting their mistresses. But for me it is impossible. You are my love, and I want you to be my wife."

"But there is something you do not know. When you discover who I am now, you may not want me at all." Kyo-no-Kimi's lips trembled and tears came to her eyes.

"Nothing you could say will change my mind," replied Yoshitsune.

"Not even if I were to tell you that I am a Heike?" Kyo-no-Kimi began to cry. "After you left, Kiyomori adopted me so that I could remain with his daughter, the ex-Empress Tokuko, safely. My father Shigeyori did not dare refuse, lest his true loyalty to Yoritomo be discovered."

Yoshitsune was clearly startled. His marrying a daughter of the Heike would trouble Yoritomo. But it was such a relief to discover that Kyo-no-Kimi's secret was no worse than that, he laughed aloud.

"Is that all?" he said. "If there's going to be trouble, we'll face it when the time comes. But nothing in the world could stop me from having you."

He turned to Kyo-no-Kimi's ladies and ordered them to prepare their mistress.

"Don't be afraid," Yoshitsune whispered to Kyo-no-Kimi. "I've arranged for a lovely house just at the edge of the city. Benkei has seen to everything, and even now a priest awaits us. In an hour you shall be my wife. Are you very frightened?"

She gazed up at him with shining eyes, smiled, and shook her head.

The marriage ceremony performed by the Shinto priest was lovely. Seaweed and peach blossoms, symbols of happiness, together with the pine, plum, and bamboo for longevity and success, were placed in the alcove, and the sacred sake cups for the marriage vows were of the finest red and gold lacquer. It was a charming and reverent ceremony, and Yoshitsune knew all the happiness that he had ever dreamed of or imagined was his.

The following days, which they spent together, were full of joy. Yoshitsune prized not only his wife's beauty, but the patience with which she had waited for him and the courage with which she had followed him. She had a quick mind as well, and often beat him at games of draughts or word-picking. She showed him scrolls which she had painted herself, and stories she had written. Under the Fujiwara, Yoshitsune knew, it had been women who had produced the greatest literature; Lady Murasaki's *Tale of Genji* and Sei Shōnagon's *Pillow Book*. And everybody at court wrote poems, love letters, and diaries. So Yoshitsune was not surprised that Kyo-no-Kimi should have an elegant hand and a flair for tales. But few ladies were talented enough to produce such works of art as Kyo-no-Kimi had done, and Yoshitsune was quite dazzled.

"Let me send some of your paintings to Goshirakawa with our wedding announcement," Yoshitsune asked to the delight of Kyo-no-Kimi.

Their days together passed quickly, and then suddenly it was time for them to return to court.

# Kyoto

It was Yoshitsune's surprise for his wife that she would not have to return to the palace. Goshirakawa turned out to be not at all displeased with their marriage, and the ex-empress graciously released Kyo-no-Kimi from her duties.

"I have arranged for a house in the third ward for us, and Benkei has already moved most of our belongings. You shall have whatever you wish."

When they arrived in their new home, dozens of messages awaited Yoshitsune and many pressing affairs.

Tadanobu was pacing impatiently back and forth in Yoshitsune's apartments in the western wing of the house. As Yoshitsune's highest ranking officer, he had been left in charge of the men.

"It was a good idea of yours to have the men camp outside the city," said Tadanobu. "They are still in good training and not wasting their energy on pleasure. But they are getting restless. And Noriyori, with Kajiwara's help, is stirring up trouble. The men are beginning to take sides. I'm glad to say that only a few side with Noriyori, but everybody wonders what is to happen next."

"This will have to stop," said Yoshitsune, his eyes hard. "A divided command is impossible. In battle, the men pay no attention to him. But here he will strut among them and persuade them that I am deserting my men for the court."

"Most of them understand what you are trying to do," said Tadanobu. "But I'm afraid of too many months of idleness."

"So am I," replied Yoshitsune. "And I wanted to attack the Heike quickly, too. But there's nothing I can do until I receive Yoritomo's reply."

"Reply?"

Yoshitsune nodded. "As soon as we arrived I sent a messenger with a long report on all that had happened." He paused. "I ended it with a request that Yoritomo relieve Noriyori of the command and make me commander-in-chief so that I could have free rein without having to worry about Noriyori's cowardice. I expect the answer any day now."

Tadanobu hesitated a moment before he said, "And what if the reply is not what you expect?"

Yoshitsune's eyes narrowed. "I think you know."

Tadanobu nodded. "We are with you," he said abruptly.

Yoshitsune laid his hand on his friend's arm. There was no need for words. Each perfectly understood the other.

"And in the meantime?" asked Tadanobu.

"I have requested an audience with Goshirakawa," said Yoshitsune. "We shall see what can be done in that quarter."

"Good. I can tell the men that they won't have to wait long."

They sat down to talk further.

"Congratulations," Tadanobu smiled. "I understand you have one of the most beautiful and accomplished wives in all Japan."

"Thank you," said Yoshitsune. "Now tell me the news about the others."

"Tsugunobu has gone to spend a few days with his old friend Saigyo in the Eastern Hills. As for Kijiro, he is simply enjoying himself. I understand he paid a visit to old Sochi and his granddaughter Nobuko."

Yoshitsune smiled, remembering the little girl who had led him through the streets of the city years before.

"Nobuko has grown up. In fact, Kijiro seems to pay her more attention than he pays Sochi."

"He won't be able to trifle with Sochi's granddaughter," said Yoshitsune, laughing. "I hope he knows what he's doing. For Kijiro to be caught in marriage would be an event." Yoshitsune paused. "And Kisanta?"

"He moons around for his wife. But he won a poetry prize the other day, and the court ladies make a fuss over him," said Tadanobu. "There is another old friend of yours who has promised to pay you a visit soon. Konnomaru. Do you remember him?"

"How could I forget? I have much to thank him for."

"He's quite an old man now, but sharp as always."

"You haven't mentioned my mother," said Yoshitsune anxiously. "Have you any news of her? I must go to see her soon."

"I went round myself to see. Very little has changed. She lives quietly. Goshirakawa has made her an allowance, and she plans to retire to a temple on Mount Hiei. She is waiting only to see you once more before she goes."

Little had changed about the old house near the Kamo River on First Avenue. The house was more dilapidated, the garden wilder, and more lonely. The roots of the tall-stemmed forest trees were choked with weeds and the brier roses overgrown in tangled hedges. Not a single spray of blossoms was to be found.

The banging of a shutter reminded him of that long ago night when he had visited her. There was not a sound in the bare and dusty house as he wandered through the rooms. Then he heard a faint rustling from behind one of the screens.

"Is someone there?" he called out.

A muffled voice responded after a long silence. "You? Can . . . it . . . be . . . you . . . my Ushiwaka?"

The sound of his childhood name flooded him with memories.

"Mother!" Yoshitsune rushed forward. "Don't hide behind the screen. Come out so that I may see how you look."

"You must not ask me to do that," came the halting voice. "You would no longer recognize me, and I want you to remember me as I was. Only tell me, how are you, my son? What has happened to you during all these years? I hear you have become the greatest warrior in the land, and that people speak of you from the rising to the setting of the sun."

"I have done what must be done." And Yoshitsune told her as much as he could. "But more important, mother, I want you to know that I shall look after you now. You shall have a pretty house and servants and everything you have lacked for the past years."

"No, Ushiwaka. I have only waited to see you once more before I leave. I have taken my vows and shall now go to the mountains to live the rest of my days in peace. Do not ask me to remain in the world. It has been too much for me."

Yoshitsune was wise enough not to argue. He understood only too well the bitterness and loneliness of his mother's life.

"Then I will provide for every comfort in your retreat. Just let me know when you wish to leave, and I shall see that all is taken care of."

"For that I thank you, Ushiwaka," she said simply.

Saddened and depressed, Yoshitsune left.

In no mood to present himself at court, Yoshitsune went home to be comforted by Kyo-no-Kimi's love.

The following morning, Yoshitsune presented himself at the Cloister Palace for his audience with Goshirakawa. He was not kept waiting, and shortly found himself seated near the dias in the main hall. Goshirakawa was holding audience with the eight ministers of state. It was a matter of the highest importance: Whom were they to acknowledge as the reigning emperor? Antoku, held by the Heike? Or Go-Toba, placed on the throne by the dead Yoshinaka of the Genji?

Goshirakawa had known for some time that a decision had to be made. But he had been waiting for the political fog to clear before he made a move. He knew the day of the Heike was over; that it was only a matter of time before the Genji clan was supreme. But there were two things he was not yet sure about. The first question was how the Genji felt toward the imperial throne itself, considering all the governmental changes they wished to make. But the second, and more immediate question, was his personal backing among the Genji.

The audience with his eight ministers was at length finished. Goshirakawa greeted Yoshitsune.

"Let us retire to more comfortable rooms where we shall have privacy to discuss certain matters."

"Excellent," agreed Yoshitsune. "We both understand what must be settled immediately."

# Decisions

The apartments through which Yoshitsune was led were the most exquisite in Kyoto. As Fujiwaras had always been, Goshirakawa was a great patron of the arts.

It occurred to Yoshitsune as they passed through the sumptuous rooms overlooking elegant gardens and shining lotus pools that Goshirakawa had been born into the wrong century. A hundred years before, he might have been the greatest of his clan. But now the land needed a change, and it was too late. Yoshitsune wondered whether Goshirakawa himself realized how hopeless it was for him to try to regain his supremacy.

As if he had read his guest's thoughts, Goshirakawa smiled and said, "When the men are there, good government will flourish, but when the men are gone, good government decays and becomes extinct. Confucius was wise in his words." Gesturing mildly with his hand, he continued, "Yet it is a pity that all this should pass."

"Though you admit the necessity for a new order of things."

"I admit the necessity," came the wry answer.

"But refinement need not be lost just because the political order changes," said Yoshitsune.

140

Goshirakawa shook his head. "You will have no time for such things. There will be too much else to attend to. Cultivation requires leisure."

They came to a large, airy room which opened out onto an enchanting landscape carefully arranged to include the faraway vista of the Eastern Hills. Little maids in gauze mantles and silken tunics scurried about preparing food, and the two men sat down to talk.

"The imperial throne cannot be left vacant much longer," said the ex-emperor. "It creates disorder. Naturally, the emperor is too young to rule, but the imperial seal is needed on laws and proclamations. And then there are rituals and religious rites for which the emperor's presence is necessary."

Yoshitsune was quick to understand what was involved for Goshirakawa. Like all Fujiwaras before him, Goshirakawa found it easier to rule through the mouth of the young emperor than to give orders as coming directly from himself. Nevertheless, it was true that the emperor must be returned to the throne.

"You are right, of course," said Yoshitsune. "The matter has been in my mind from the first. And in Yoritomo's. We fully understand the importance of returning the Emperor Antoku to his proper throne."

"Then his young brother, Go-Toba, is not to be invested?"

"It was not up to Yoshinaka to make and unmake emperors. Antoku is still the emperor of Japan and must be taken from the Heike."

Goshirakawa nodded.

By now Yoshitsune fully realized that Goshirakawa meant to support the Genji, and he did not hesitate therefore to make his request.

"Yoritomo's fleet has embarked from Kamakura. I am in hopes that it will arrive shortly. But I want to attack the Heike quickly. Will you put your ships at my disposal?"

If the suddenness of Yoshitsune's request startled Goshirakawa, he betrayed nothing. But his reply was evasive.

"I will see what can be done. My hands are somewhat tied, you understand, and certain things may be very difficult."

Yoshitsune's quick mind missed nothing. So Goshirakawa suspected Yoritomo's mixed feelings for his brother. A sense of futility swept over Yoshitsune. Why should Yoritomo do this to him? All he wanted was for Yoritomo's own good. Now, there was nothing he could do but wait for Yoritomo's reply. Should he, Yoshitsune, be made commander-in-chief and be put in full charge of affairs at the capital, all would be well. If not, he would have to consider well what was to be done.

When the letter came from the east it was short. The messenger who carried it was none other than Shigeyori, Yoshitsune's father-in-law, whom Yoritomo had recalled to Kamakura. Yoshitsune read the letter quickly and, pale with anger, flung it down.

"What is the meaning of this?" he demanded furiously. "Why should Yoritomo distrust me so much that he appoints Noriyori commander-in-chief instead of me? And on top of that, to give command of the fleet to that Heike traitor Kajiwara? Why? Doesn't he know that I can end this war quickly for him? And that the others will merely play cat and mouse with the enemy? Surely he lacks not only loyalty in this but wisdom!"

Shigeyori stared into the angry eyes and at the set jaw which flung these words at him from across the room. He matched with equal coldness the hot fury of Yoshitsune.

"I have only this to say," he began icily. "Yoritomo wishes you to return to Kamakura. He suspects you not only as a rival, but as a traitor."

Yoshitsune's amazement and hurt overcame his anger. "What do you say?" His voice was a hoarse whisper. "A traitor?"

He was speechless. What under all the heavens could he reply to such an accusation? Could Yoritomo really stoop so low?

But why? It had never occurred to him for a moment to oppose his brother. All he wanted was to devote himself to his duties and the honor of the Genji, to the support of his elder brother. Surely Yoritomo could not be so blind as to imagine Yoshitsune guilty of wanting to overthrow him. What on earth could have brought this insult to pass?

Yoshitsune was startled by the sound of Shigeyori's voice answering. He must have spoken his last thought aloud.

"You have asked Goshirakawa for his support should you decide to overthrow Yoritomo."

"Yoritomo cannot believe that. I have enlisted Goshirakawa's support for his sake, not my own," replied Yoshitsune simply.

"You married a daughter of the Heike," continued Shigeyori stubbornly.

Yoshitsune's voice was cold then. The last accusation was too outrageous to take seriously.

"You, of all people, to stand there and make such a statement," he said quietly. "I simply cannot believe I need remind you that Kyo-no-Kimi is your own daughter. And that it was you who permitted her adoption into the Heike clan to suit your own convenience. And need I remind my brother that he himself took a wife from the house of Hojo, vassals to the Heike? Shigeyori, this is growing ridiculous."

Shigeyori was silent.

Yoshitsune strode across the room and faced him squarely.

"You are afraid to say these things to Yoritomo for fear of losing his favor."

Shigeyori stiffened. "What reply shall I bring Yoritomo?" was all he said.

Yoshitsune's anger returned. "You may tell him that I have no intention of returning to Kamakura. This quarreling has lost us a great deal of time already, and the Heike gain in strength with every day that passes. I shall remain here to stick thorns into Noriyori until he decides to make a move."

Yoshitsune paused and swallowed hard. "And since Yoritomo has so decreed that Noriyori is first in command, I shall pledge him my support." Yoshitsune fingered his sword. "And tell my brother Yoritomo," he said bitterly, "that he shall have his kingdom in spite of himself."

# The Battle of Yashima

Throughout the spring and summer Yoshitsune urged and goaded Noriyori to take action. The longer they waited to attack, the stronger the Heike grew and the more supporters they gained.

"It is being rumored that we are afraid, that we are finished," said Tadanobu angrily. "The men begin to wonder whether they have come all this way for nothing."

"I know," replied Yoshitsune somberly.

"I understand your duty to your brother and that you don't want to override those he has placed in charge."

"Families are not made strong by divided factions. Once before the Genji were divided, and my father's death and the supremacy of the Heike was the result."

"You are only arguing with a decision you have already made," said Tadanobu.

Yoshitsune smiled at his friend's quick understanding. "Yes, it is different this time. I fight for, not against, Yoritomo, though he cannot seem to see it. My brother is wise, and yet it is strange that he does not understand this. I have no choice but to override Noriyori and Kajiwara. The cause of the Genji is at stake. My only hope is that Yoritomo will forgive what I do."

On a ridge high in the Eastern Hills, a lone figure in the robes of a monk stood outlined against the glow of the early evening. In the young face the eyes were thoughtful, and the man listened to the wind in the pines once more before he wound his way down to the bamboo hut.

"I must leave tomorrow morning," said Tsugunobu quietly.

"So soon?" Saigyo's voice was troubled. "I will die before long. I had hoped to hear you take your vows."

Tsugunobu was silent a moment. In the hauntingly lovely evening he heard the distant cry of an owl. "So I had thought," he said after a while. "But the time has not yet come. I must join Yoshitsune tomorrow. And when it is all over—when it is over I shall return to you here. On this mountain, in this hut is all I have ever wished for."

Saigyo nodded. "You must go. So long as worldly matters weigh on you, you cannot attain peace. Yet these wars are madness. In the end it will not matter." Saigyo paused. "And yet, in spite of myself, I have great sympathy for Yoshitsune. He hasn't the foresight nor the patience of Yoritomo. He is not the greater ruler—yet he is the greater man. That is why I fear for him. Yoritomo is jealous of the very life in his younger brother, which he has quelled in himself. Yoshitsune will win his battles for him and then . . ."

"And then?"

"He who asks and receives another's help becomes his slave. Gratitude is the most unbearable of all emotions. I fear less for Yoshitsune's life in battle than I do in the hands of his elder brother. Yoritomo is a great and wise man. His only flaw is his feelings toward his brother. If he could overcome this, he would be unique among men," said Saigyo.

"Had the brothers been born one man! Yoshitsune's humanity with Yoritomo's wisdom . . ."

"We should have had a Buddha for a king, and that is too much perfection for this world to cope with. Sometimes I think we only love each other for our failings. Yet our goal is the Buddhahood, the very perfection we cannot live with."

"Strange talk from a monk," said Tsugunobu.

"I begin to believe in mercy," replied Saigyo, "not perfection."

"Do come," urged Kisanta. "We are late already."

In the gay, lantern-lit garden, Kijiro clasped Nobuko's hands. "I shall soon return," he said. Nobuko brushed the flowered sleeves of her kimono across her eyes and her lips trembled. Then she smiled, so Kijiro would not have a sorrowful memory of her. "It is not the arrows of the warriors I fear, but the pretty ladies."

"Never," protested Kijiro. "Your grandfather has promised you to me, you delightful creature, and I shall be back for you." They both knew he would keep his promise.

Following Kisanta, Kijiro left quickly. The two made their way along the Kamo River's willow-edged bank toward the home of their chieftain.

Noriyori paced back and forth in his room and came to a halt in front of Yoshitsune.

"I forbid you to go," asserted Noriyori importantly. "After all, I am in command here, and I shall decide when the time has come to attack."

Yoshitsune was silent. They had been through this so many times before, that further discussion seemed pointless. Kajiwara stared at him with steely eyes, daring Yoshitsune to make his move. He laughed harshly.

"You will need ships. I understand Goshirakawa has so far given you none. Just where do you propose to get them?"

Yoshitsune wheeled to face Noriyori and Kajiwara. He spoke furiously between clenched teeth. "You are blind and incompetent fools. I shall argue no more."

He crossed the room, and gripping the handle of his sword,

paused for a moment before leaving.

"But do not look for me in the morning. With or without your consent, I travel south tomorrow."

At the Hour of the Tiger the rising sun glinted on eighty helmets and on the shining manes of eighty war horses as Yoshitsune led his small contingent south from the capital to the shores of the Inland Sea. They camped on the beach near Naniwa on the evening of the following day.

The Heike fleet, on which the entire Heike army was to embark, lay across the straits, sheltered in the bay of Yashima off the island of Shikoku. Yashima was a narrow peninsula not far from the island's main town of Takamatsu. The waters nearby were treacherous with strong currents and small rocky islets easy enough to miss, against which a ship could be smashed to pieces.

"It might be difficult to swim," commented Benkei wryly. His powerful arms gleamed in the firelight as he polished the hilt of his sword.

The Sato brothers and the Yoshioka brothers looked up as Yoshitsune came from his tent with a map of the straits and Shikoku Island.

"I wouldn't mind giving the five of you a good dousing," he said, "but I would not dream of doing that to the horses. Black Lacquer has been too good a friend." Then his face grew serious. "In spite of Kajiwara's opposition, I have managed to persuade the captains of five of the ships to take us across."

"That is not very many," commented Tadanobu.

"Neither are we," added Kijiro.

But they were merely making conversation. Such was their faith in Yoshitsune that they had little doubt of success. Even with a third the number of their forces, they knew that if Yoshitsune led them, victory was theirs. And even if they doubted, such was their loyalty to him that they would have followed him even to certain death.

"The ships are ready. We have only to wait for a storm," said Yoshitsune evenly.

Benkei gasped. "A storm! You cannot mean to say that you actually want a storm to travel across those straits."

Yoshitsune nodded. "I admit it is an enormous risk. But without a storm it will not even be a question of risk. It would be certain death."

Even Tadanobu shook his head in bewilderment.

"First of all, the crossing normally takes three days. With the blasting wind of an autumn storm, we should be able to make the crossing in six or eight hours. Speed is necessary. The Heike are thousands strong against our eighty. The faster we go, the less chance of their knowing of our arrival. Second, they will hardly expect an attack in stormy weather. They will sit in their Bay of Yashima thoroughly secure, positive that we could not possibly make it without several days of good weather. Speed and surprise will make the odds a little more even."

"You are out of your mind," said Benkei, "but you are absolutely right."

They did not have long to wait. By early morning a heavy storm had begun to brew. Dark, swollen clouds buffeted each other across a restless sky and the shrill cries of the wild birds pierced the rising howl of the winds.

"To the ships! To the ships!"

Orders were screamed against the rushing air, and the beach resounded with the pounding of horses hooves as they were ridden across the sands and into the shallows to the five ships anchored close to the shore. The wind had been blowing from the east; but by the time the ships were ready to draw anchor, it had shifted until it was directly behind them, heaving them straight out to sea.

"Even the elements are with us," howled Benkei in glee.

A wild exultation filled them all. The air was silver; electric with a power that would soon explode in a torrent of rain. The

men were gleeful. The rains came, and the wind hurried them
onward across the Inland Sea. The expert captains knew the
straits and guided the ships among the jutting rocks that dotted
their path. The ships sped on, hour after hour, the wind at their
backs. It was a dangerous undertaking, but at the helm of the
lead ship, Yoshitsune seemed to draw them on by the power of
his will. From time to time the rains lessened, but the day was
dark as night, and under cover of the storm the small Genji force
approached its destination in enemy territory.

It was already night, when, with a last fierce surge of violence,
the wind pushed them ashore. They landed on a deserted strip
of coast on the island of Shikoku not many miles from Yashima.

They neither desired nor needed rest; and secretly, riding by

night, the small band made its way around the island. Yoshitsune paused just outside of the neighboring town of Takamatsu and held up his war fan as a signal to halt. Tadanobu rode up to his side.

"Why do we stop?"

"Our success depends now on frightening the Heike army into thinking there are many more of us than there are. If they thought we were only eighty, they would simply attack and massacre us. They must be persuaded that we are hundreds more, so that they will take to their ships. It will be easier to set fire to the ships than to attempt an attack on their land camp."

"How do you plan to turn eighty men into an army?"

"Bring Tsugunobu and Benkei and follow me."

The four men rode swiftly toward Takamatsu. Yoshitsune knew that the islanders had not taken kindly to the Heike occupation and secretly were sympathetic to the Genji. The four rode hurriedly into town.

In half an hour the town looked as though it were ablaze. The people, only too happy to help the Genji, had collected brushwood and started great bonfires. They raised such a tumult of shouting and screaming and wailing that it echoed down the shore to where the Heike army was encamped.

The effect on the Heike was instantaneous. The great blaze was their first warning of the coming of the Genji; and from the tremendous havoc they saw and heard, the Heike could only assume that they were being attacked by a great host. In a panic, the entire camp broke and took to their ships, exactly as Yoshitsune had predicted. Horses broke loose, tents were overturned, armor was tramped underfoot, confused orders were unheard or unheeded as the terrified army raced pell-mell into the sea.

Tadanobu brought the rest of the eighty horsemen down to the beach at full speed. Yoshitsune divided them into small groups and sent them racing up and down the shore in every direction, shouting and yelling to each other at the tops of their voices, galloping back and forth on the turf and kicking up a violent spray in the water.

Yoshitsune had also commandeered a large herd of bullocks and had ordered that flaring torches be lashed to their horns. Now, screaming them into a frenzy, he sent them pounding down the beach and through the water until the tumult rose to an unearthly roar.

He raced out onto the beach and yelled his own name and honors and any others he could think of. His horsemen followed suit. The Heike, by this time thoroughly convinced that an enormous army surrounded them, cowered in their ships.

"How long can we manage to fool them?" gasped Benkei, riding up to Yoshitsune's side. "The men are getting tired and cannot go on much longer."

"Even more serious," replied Yoshitsune, "is that soon the Heike will expect an attack. After all this havoc, they will hardly believe we simply plan to scream at them all night."

They worried none too soon. But by the time the Heike discovered that they outnumbered the attacking Genji by more than twenty to one, it was too late to retrieve their position. Instead, a contingent of five hundred of the Heike left their ships and managed to land in spite of Genji attempts to beat them back into the sea.

But by this time the Genji were slowly but steadily being joined by groups of sympathizers. Word had been sent around the island. Even some of the Heike forces came over to their side. The battling armies were still far from equal. But the Genji were a little stronger, and in a better position for attack.

"Had you counted on this?" asked Tsugunobu.

"I knew we had allies on the island, or I would not have risked all our lives coming here. Now that our forces have grown, we can take better advantage of the situation."

Yoshitsune whipped his horse around and yelled to Tadanobu. "We still don't have enough men or ships to beat them completely, but if we can just push them out to sea and cut off their line of supply, we can weaken them for a future final attack. Have we enough men to accomplish it, do you think?"

"That was no question," said Tadanobu, grinning. "That, my lord, was an order."

The battle was heaviest farther down the beach, and the three, joined by Benkei, Kijiro, and Kisanta, rode into the thick of it.

When the Heike bowmen caught sight of Yoshitsune, they concentrated all their fury on him alone. If Yoshitsune could be killed, so could the spirit of the Genji army. Destroy Yoshitsune, and the Genji army would melt away.

"Look!"

Benkei's eyes followed Tsugunobu's pointing finger. Yoshitsune, engaged in furious combat with several Heike soldiers, was unaware of what was happening a dozen yards behind him. The Heike bowmen were quieting their horses in order to take perfect aim. Faster than the eye could see, Tsugunobu and Tadanobu, Kisanta and Kijiro, and Benkei, gathering twelve or fourteen others on their way, were at Yoshitsune's side. Together they formed a living shield before their lord to save his life. As they formed the shield, they drew their bows and the shafts flew through the air. The Genji drove the Heike bowmen back; but before they did, the Heike had had time to take careful aim. In their midst was the best of the Heike archers, Noritsune, whose shaft never missed.

Ten of the bodyguard around Yoshitsune fell, and among them was Tsugunobu. When he saw Noritsune take aim, he reined in his horse and threw himself directly in front of his lord. He fell to the ground, pierced by an arrow. Horrified, Yoshitsune leaped from his horse. Cradling Tsugunobu in his arms in the midst of the battling soldiers, he wept, forgetting his own safety and the glittering swords threatening from all sides.

"Ah, my Tsugunobu, not you. Why you, of all of us? Surely none has led a purer, more devoted life."

Tsugunobu's voice was hoarse, and he spoke with difficulty. "May the Amida Buddha bless you and keep you safe, my lord. Say to Saigyo . . ."

"Don't try to speak. I understand what you would wish me to say. It shall be done."

And with his master's arm about him, Tsugunobu died. Yoshitsune's shoulders shook with sobs. He raised his eyes to Tadanobu.

"And all he wanted was a simple hut in the hills and time for his music and his meditations." His glance returned to the pure and peaceful face of his friend. "Go now, Tsugunobu," he whispered. "Go to your home in the Eastern Hills."

His soldiers, watching their master, were moved. One of them said, "For the sake of a lord like this, who would consider his life more than dust or dew?"

Again and again the Heike attempted to drive off the Genji hosts, only to be forced to retreat into the sea. Finally, a charge of Genji horsemen, headed by Yoshitsune himself, blind with anger and sorrow, furiously drove the Heike before them and sent them flying headlong back to their ships. Like the demon spirit of the Tengu, Yoshitsune charged, and none remained standing where he rode. Amid the salt spray, swords clashing in their hands, they pursued the Heike until they were up to their saddles in the sea.

"Don't stop," shouted Yoshitsune, enraged against the entire Heike army for the death of one of his dearest friends and followers. "Come ahead, after me."

After him they came, to throw flaring torches against the Heike ships.

When the dawn arrived, clear and chill, the battle was over. The Heike had been forced to leave the sheltered anchorage of Yashima Bay and put to sea. It was all over; the Genji had won.

Wearily, Yoshitsune returned to the shore. The five gathered around the motionless form of Tsugunobu to mourn.

"Let us have him taken back to the hills," said Yoshitsune quietly. "It is all we can do for him now, and I think it would please him."

"Thank you," whispered Tadanobu, his face ashen with grief. "The hills will accept his silent vows."

# Dan No Ura

Yoshitsune walked silently along the rim of the sea. The lonely voice of a crane dissolved in the gray mist as it rose above the rushes, and the crickets were hushed beneath the clear autumn moon.

A tired loneliness welled up within him. Lying back on the sand, he longed for Kyo-no-Kimi with all of the need for love that was part of his nature. He stared up at the sky and was reminded of the ancient legend of the Weaver Princess and the Herdboy. So much in love were they that she had neglected her weaving and he his cows. To punish them, her father the Celestial King had forced them apart, each on the opposite side of the Milky Way. He said they could meet once a year—but there was no bridge across the stars. The magpies, seeing their sorrow, took pity on them. Once a year they spread their wings to form a bridge for the lovers to cross.

As he thought of the story, a chill struck Yoshitsune's heart. He remembered Yoritomo's ill will toward him. For himself, he could bear exile or an honorable death. It was Kyo-no-Kimi who would suffer. How could she stand the hardships of exile? And should he die, what would become of her? No magpie alive dared cross Yoritomo's anger to form a bridge between them.

And how long would it be before the rest of the Genji army arrived? He had sent messages reporting their success to Noriyori and Yoritomo and asked for troops and ships. Until they arrived, all Yoshitsune could do was guard the beach position and keep the Heike from landing.

The night mist lay heavy over the garden. Kyo-no-Kimi opened the sliding screen and watched the fireflies dart amid the clumps of Chinese bamboo. A book of love poems by poetess Ono-no-Komachi rested in her slender hands. As she waited alone through the cool days and the dew-drenched nights for the coming of Yoshitsune, two of the poems floated often through her mind.

> *This night of no moon*
> *There is no way to meet him.*
> *I rise in longing—*
> *My breast pounds, a leaping flame,*
> *My heart is consumed in fire.*

And of the other she could remember only the first three lines.

> *So lonely am I.*
> *My body is a floating weed*
> *Severed at the roots. . . .*

How she needed him and missed him. They had had so little time together. They loved, she knew, in a way that would have made them happy to grow old together. Yet if it was not to be . . . Though Yoshitsune had never told her, Kyo-no-Kimi had lived too long at court not to know the ways of the world and how difficult things could be.

Silently, she watched the sinking moon. Her eyes widened, and she gave a small cry of delight. For the first time in months she dared to hope again. In swift joy, she placed her hand underneath her sash to feel the first fluttering of life. She knew she was carrying his child.

During the following days Yoshitsune had little time to spare for personal thoughts. With his usual about-face, Noriyori had applauded Yoshitsune's success, and with Yoritomo's approval, set out with the entire Genji army and a large fleet of ships to join Yoshitsune. Now a full effort was to be made to overcome the Heike and return the emperor and the three imperial regalia to Kyoto. Yoshitsune, thrilled at the thought of a complete and final victory, collected his army and made ready to cross over to Dan no Ura to join forces with Kajiwara and Noriyori.

Tadanobu entered the tent where Benkei was busily packing and polishing armor.

"Where is Yoshitsune?"

"At the shrine offering prayers to the god Hachiman."

Tadanobu looked surprised. "But he hasn't visited a shrine or a temple since his days at the monastery."

Benkei's powerful arms hoisted a heavy trunk outside the tent.

"There comes a time in a man's life when he wants every power he can think of on his side," Benkei said. "He has just gotten a letter from Kyo-no-Kimi. She is with child. He's been like an excited child himself over the news. So he went off to pray to the guardian god of the Genji, the great Hachiman, for a swift battle and a swifter return."

"Which shrine did he go to? Which way did he take?" Clearly, Tadanobu was worried.

Benkei shrugged. "How should I know? Shikoku is the island of temples and shrines—hundreds of them as far as the eye can see. And since this is the season for pilgrimages, the place is packed. You will hardly find him in this throng."

"I must try."

"Is it something urgent?"

"Kyo-no-Kimi is in danger. The ex-Empress Tokuko has fled from court to join her son Antoku. Without her protection, Kyo-no-Kimi is alone. Noriyori might think to please Yoritomo by ending the marriage in some terrible way."

Benkei frowned. "It can do no good to tell Yoshitsune about it. He can't protect Kyo-no-Kimi from here, and he'll only worry himself sick. As an honorable warrior, he'll sail with the Genji. He cannot go to her. Instead, we'll send a message to Saigyo. He will do all he can to look after her."

Tadanobu nodded. "You are right. We will say nothing."

Yoshitsune threaded his way among the crowds milling in the outer court of a temple dedicated to the great ninth century priest Kobo Daishi. He had prayed to the eternal Buddha, and now he would go to a Shinto shrine.

In a few moments, Yoshitsune passed under the great wooden *tori*, the gate to every Shinto shrine, hung with the *shimenawa*, the sacred rope. He purified his mouth and hands, rinsing them with water at the well, and moved toward the shrine itself. Removing his gold horned helmet, he bowed, kneeled, and clapped his hands to call for the god's attention. Then he made his offering of rice wine.

"May the gods protect you better than they did your father," said a somber voice behind him. "We go with you in spirit, young man."

Yoshitsune smiled at the priest in his flowing robes and bowed his thanks.

"One of your men awaits you just beyond the gate."

Yoshitsune bowed again and hurried outside to find Tadanobu and Benkei anxiously searching for his face in the crowds.

"Ah, there you are."

"Is it time?"

"All is ready."

"Then let us go."

❀ ❀ ❀

The great hosts of the Genji and the Heike faced each other across the waters just off the coast of Dan no Ura and prepared to engage, ship to ship.

Pale, already defeated in his soul, the great Heike general Munemori paced the deck of his vessel.

"Your final orders, my lord?" requested Tomomori, equally pale and shaken.

"This time they outnumber us," said Munemori quietly. "Not that it makes any difference. Even when ours was the larger force, we were beaten. Our time has come, that is all. The light of the Heike flickers and grows dim, while the flame of the Genji soars into the heavens. All things are born and pass away, only to be born again in the endless flow of eternity. The sun of Buddha's wisdom lights a thousand worlds and he is merciful. We will bend as the willows in his wind."

"There is no hope?"

"It is not our armor, but our spirits that are weak. Today's battle was lost a long time ago." Munemori let the salt spray lash his face. The taste of the salt was bitter. "Our only hope lies in an honorable death. We have nothing more to give our land. We have grown old," he said and added wryly, "The land needs a younger strength. It is a time not for moon viewing, but for the harvesting of rice."

Munemori turned abruptly, straightening his sword in its brocaded sash. "See that the Emperor Antoku, his mother, and grandmother remain below. Are the soldiers divided as I commanded?"

Tomomori nodded. "Our best warriors are aboard the ordinary warships, and our weaker warriors on the big ships of Chinese build."

"The Genji will attack the large ships first. It will give us a chance to surround them and attack from behind with our finest archers. They will think they are winning easily and it will make them overconfident. Then if we can just manage to take Yoshitsune from them . . ."

"What if the emperor should fall into their hands?"

Munemori was silent for a moment. "In truth, I don't know. I understand Yoritomo has the greatest respect for the imperial throne. And yet, Antoku is after all the grandson of Kiyomori. Yoritomo may not want an emperor with Heike blood. It is hard to say."

A commotion in the ship's bow interrupted them. The Genji fleet had been spotted. The Heike ships lined up and leveled hundreds of arrows. They were ready and waiting.

"We are strong," said Tadanobu with satisfaction. "The men of Shikoku and the southern island of Kyushu have joined us. Kajiwara is behind us with the entire Genji fleet, and Noriyori has the army on the beach to catch any Heike who try to escape to shore."

"The battle isn't won yet," replied Yoshitsune. "Genji horsemanship is fine, but the Heike know better than we how to fight by sea."

"Here they come!"

The cry was taken up and yelled back and forth among the ships. The tide brought the vessels swiftly together, and a rain of arrows sped across the waters. Both sides faced each other grimly, with no thought for their individual lives.

"The Heike fight hard," grunted Benkei, drawing another shaft.

"They're fighting to protect the emperor and the three sacred treasures. It gives them courage," returned Kisanta, whose perfect aim brought down a foe with each arrow.

Kajiwara was bringing his fleet around to close in on a direct attack on the largest among the Heike warships.

"Let him have the honor of subduing their greatest generals and warriors," said Yoshitsune gravely. "Order our helmsmen to steer toward the smaller ships."

Tadanobu was angry. "Why leave such an honor to that scoundrel? It should be yours."

"It is the honor of the Genji that matters, not my own." Yoshitsune's voice was grim. "Do as I say."

The ships were brought around and moved in. Suddenly Yoshitsune's fleet received the shock of an attack by the finest and bravest of the Heike. Having shot a battery of arrows, the Heike swarmed over the sides of the Genji ships. Yoshitsune realized right away what Munemori had done, but it was too late. Overwhelmed in numbers, the Genji fought against the outraged Heike war lords, ready to die or win in one last vicious attack. The Heike champions struck and struck again. Coming between Kajiwara and Yoshitsune, the Heike divided the Genji fleet. Swords glittered and clashed, and arrows blackened the sky.

Panting with exhaustion, fighting for his life every inch of the way, Yoshitsune managed to reach Tadanobu.

"Follow me."

Collecting several more warriors in his wake, Yoshitsune made his way to the back of his doomed warship and lowered a small boat.

"We have only a few minutes before they notice I am gone," he said quickly. "There is only one way to stop this attack. A moment ago, I caught sight of the emperor on that ship." His finger indicated the direction. "If we can get to the ship and try to take the emperor, the Heike will stop their attack in order to defend him from us. Our men will be given time to catch their breaths, and Kajiwara will have a chance to break through and join our ships."

"Excellent," said Benkei. "But will you please stay behind and hide yourself? We cannot afford to lose you, and this small boat gives no protection at all."

Yoshitsune grinned. "Stop being an old nursemaid and get this boat going."

Partly hidden by the side of the warship, partly by the Heike's concentration on the battle at hand, they managed to row the boat to the waters near the ship that carried the emperor.

"They have left the ship unprotected," gasped Tadanobu. "Not a single warrior aboard save for a few old guards."

It was too late to stop what happened next. Those of the Heike who turned in time gasped in horror.

The Lady Nii, grandmother to the emperor, had already decided what she would do if any of the Genji came near the ship. She had been able to see the whole of the battle and knew that in spite of the temporary Heike attack, the Genji fleet could not be withstood for long; already the Heike were weakening. And she saw Kajiwara, who had by then beaten the warriors on the big ships, approaching to reinforce Yoshitsune's smaller fleet. When she spied Yoshitsune himself nearing, she donned

an outer robe of dark gray mourning, and tucking up her silken skirts, placed the sacred jewel and mirror under her arm, the sacred sword in her sash, and took the young Antoku in her arms.

To the child she said, tears streaming down her cheeks, "Face the east and bid farewell to the Sun Goddess at Ise, and then the west and say the prayer that Amida Buddha may come to welcome you in Paradise."

Wonder and anxiety on his face, the young emperor said, "But where are you taking me?"

His grandmother, the widow of Kiyomori, replied, "This world is filled with sorrow now. There is a pure land of happiness beneath the waves, a land where there is no sorrow. It is there I am taking you."

The child sovereign put his hands together in prayer and smiled courageously. Lady Nii bound up his long hair in his dove-colored robe. Then holding him tightly in her arms, she said, "I am but a woman, yet I will not let our Sovereign Lord fall into the hands of the enemy. Let those of you who will, follow me. In the depths of the ocean is our capital," and sank with him at last beneath the waves.

With a cry of dismay and sorrow, the ex-Empress Tokuko, Antoku's mother, saw what had happened and followed her son and mother into the sea. Finally recovering from their shock, several sailors jumped in after them to save their lives. For the emperor and his grandmother it was too late, but they managed to save Lady Tokuko and retrieve the imperial regalia.

Yoshitsune, boarding the ship, saw too late what had happened. He stood silently for a moment, grieving for the child, then turned abruptly to give his orders.

The battle did not last long after that. Infuriated at the Heike that they should have left the emperor unguarded, Yoshitsune attacked with renewed force. Little by little the strength and spirit of the Heike failed. One after another, the great Heike generals threw themselves into the sea, the great princes of the

House of Heike preferring to die rather than fall into the hands of the enemy.

Soon the waters of the sea were red with Heike banners, like a mountain river in autumn flecked with the falling leaves of the maple; and the deserted, empty ships rocked mournfully on the waves.

# The White Banner

The moon of the seventeenth night shone softly into the rock pool of the holy man's garden. From within the hut came the sound of a lute tuned to the wind lingering in the black pines of the mountain. The music trailed away into the night, and the figure of Kyo-no-Kimi clad in a simple white underrobe appeared in the doorway, moving silently across the garden to the thatched pavilion near the stream. Gracefully she bent and cupped in slender hands a mouthful of water, and with a piece of silk moistened her brow. Entering the pavilion, she rested for a moment on a straw mat, lonely, faint with longing, waiting.

Watching her there, Yoshitsune could barely restrain himself from crying out to her. Yet having no wish to disturb those who slept within the hut, he crept noiselessly as a mountain deer toward the pavilion. Softly his arms encircled her.

"My love," he whispered.

With a little moan she sank against him, and he buried his face in her hair.

"You come to me like the wind in the night," she said. "I am not at all sure you are real."

He clasped her tightly in his arms and laughed, and their

166

joy flooded the garden with a light as clear as the moon.

After a time, she spoke again. "I have not asked—how did it go?"

He told her of the long marches, the ships at sea, all the battles and victories, and the fate of some of those she knew. She was saddened at the death of Tsugunobu and comforted Yoshitsune.

Then she asked, "The Heike are truly defeated? There will be no more war?"

"Japan is in Yoritomo's hands now," Yoshitsune replied gravely. "He will rule wisely and with justice. He will put strength and order back into the land. The peasants will have rice. And though the imperial throne will endure, the noblemen will no longer sap the country with taxes for which they make no return."

"That is well for Japan," she said quietly. "But what of you?"

Yoshitsune was startled. He had not thought she knew of what lay between himself and Yoritomo.

"I don't know," he replied. "But let's not speak of that now."

"Do not hide the truth from me. I want to know. I am not afraid." She looked with her clear eyes into his. "What shall you do now?"

"I bring him victory, and Munemori and his son as a peace offering. I want to support his reign and bring honor to the house of Genji." Then he added simply, "If Yoritomo understands this, all will be well."

"And if not? If he distrusts you and turns against you?"

He took her hands in his own strong hands. "Tell me," he said with shining eyes. "When is our child to be born?"

"In the spring," she smiled. "In the fourth month when the cherry blossoms come."

"We must return to the capital for the Ceremony of Investiture. Go-Toba is to receive the imperial crown. And then we shall wait together until the child is born before I go to Kamakura."

"So many months together?" Kyo-no-Kimi asked wonderingly. She had not dared to hope for so much.

"Sleep now," he said; and holding one another close, they slept.

The close of that year was celebrated at court with the usual New Year festivities; and at the palace, the imperial banquet was held with magnificent splendor. Visits and gifts of new clothing were exchanged, and Yoshitsune received one of the twenty-one white horses presented yearly to the emperor and afterwards given by him to members of his family and those he wished to honor. It was Goshirakawa, of course, as advisor to the child-emperor, who had seen to it that Yoshitsune was thus honored. The court made up for their sadness over the death of Antoku and the retirement of the ex-Empress Tokuko to a mountain hermitage by fêting the victorious Yoshitsune. His powerful position, as well as his gentle manners, made him a great favorite. His supremacy was accepted by nearly everyone without protest. Those Heike who were still in office resigned quietly, and there was peace in Kyoto.

Some people, those few who gave deep thought to the politi-cal situation, remained uneasy. For a while, they were pleased that the strutting Heike were gone. But then they began to hear reports about Yoritomo's plans for economic and political changes. Court officials were never happy about any sort of change, much less the huge changes they heard Yoritomo was planning. Would he really make them stop taxing the peasants as much as they wished? Would he really make the nobles leave the pleasures of court to look after their estates? Was he actually going to set up law courts for *everybody*? And what about the rumor that he planned to rule from Kamakura in the east, instead of from the western capital!

Yet for the time being all this was in the future, and the court continued its round of pleasures as usual, until the thundering voice from the east should make its wishes openly known.

Shortly after the New Year celebration, with Yoritomo's approval, Go-Toba was made emperor. The Ceremony of the Putting on of the Trousers, which marked Go-Toba's third birthday, was followed by the Ceremony of Investiture. And Go-Toba received the three imperial regalia, symbols of his succession to the throne.

Yoshitsune ruled the capital wisely. Peace and order were everywhere. Only once again did he disobey his brother's orders. He refused to carry out Yoritomo's command to kill all the surviving Heike. An ominous silence followed his refusal.

With the first clear freshets of spring flowing down from the mountains, the first pale cherry blossoms billowing in pink clouds against the sky, Kyo-no-Kimi gave to Yoshitsune his firstborn, a son. Holding the tiny infant in his arms, he knelt at his wife's side.

"Thank you," he whispered. And he lay a sprig of blossoms on her pillow.

Her lips trembled only a little as she touched his lips with her slender hand. "Go, my lord," she said. "Ride to the east. You have avenged your father's death and brought victory and honor to the clan of Genji. And may Yoritomo in all his wisdom see into your heart and grant you the honor you deserve."

With the faithful Benkei on his left, the warrior Tadanobu on his right, Yoshitsune rode eastward toward Mount Fuji. The mounted warriors had proved themselves the mightiest archers, the boldest horsemen, the most brilliant swordsmen of the land; and as their horses pounded the earth into dust, the men carried the white banner of the Genji high, lifting it proudly into the clear sky.

Yoshitsune rode before them; and in his general's armor of gold lacquer laced with silver cord, the curving sword of the warrior at his waist, he shone like the gods of his ancestors with the pride and dignity of the truly great among men.

From behind him rose a mighty roar, a pledge of eternal loyalty from the warriors to their adored and shining leader, Yoshitsune, the warlord of the House of Genji.

It was a glory too brilliant to burn for long.

Yoritomo, envious and fearful of his brother as a rival, refused to allow Yoshitsune to enter Kamakura. He was ordered to send only the prisoners, especially Munemori and his son, both of whom, against Yoshitsune's plea, Yoritomo instantly beheaded. For three weeks Yoshitsune remained in a little village about two miles from the city. He wrote a moving letter to Yoritomo; but Yoritomo remained cold and silent. There was nothing Yoshitsune could do but return with his followers to Kyoto.

From Kyoto, Yoshitsune did all he could to prevent the ruthless killing off of the Heike ordered by Yoritomo. Again he wrote his brother. Yoritomo's answer was to demand the head of Yoshitsune's Heike wife. Horrified and furious, Yoshitsune tried, with Goshirakawa's help, to put an army together to fight Yoritomo. But it was too late. Yoritomo was already marching on Kyoto. Yoshitsune fled with his wife, his son, and his small band of retainers to the hills. Goshirakawa, bending always with the strongest wind, welcomed Yoritomo and outlawed Yoshitsune.

After months of flight, hiding from Yoritomo's spies and soldiers, Yoshitsune made his way once more to Mutsu, where the Fujiwara chieftain Hidehira had once given him a home. Hidehira, now over ninety, sheltered Yoshitsune, his family, and his band in the Fujiwara castle. And then, suddenly, Hidehira died.

"We are done," said Yoshitsune simply.

"Not you, not while I live," scowled Benkei.

"Hidehira's son will betray us," Yoshitsune answered, his eyes reflecting the sad but absolute knowledge of great men.

It was early in summer, in 1189, when Hidehira's son,

threatened with death by Yoritomo if he did not act, led an army to surround the castle.

Yoshitsune, Benkei, and the small faithful band of followers defended the castle as long as they could. In rage and grief Yoshitsune fought, watching the friends who had been with him so long fall in the hopeless battle.

By evening, though the men had killed hundreds of the enemy, only Yoshitsune and Benkei were left. Bloodstained, his huge form shaking with exhaustion, Benkei cried out to his master in a hoarse but still gentle voice.

"Escape, my lord. Take Kyo-no-Kimi and your son. I will hold them off a little longer."

Yoshitsune shook his head and entered the castle. In an inner room sat Kyo-no-Kimi. On her lap was the dead body of their son. They exchanged a long look. Yoshitsune knew what would happen to her if Yoritomo took her alive.

"I want to be with you," she whispered.

He took her in his arms, drew his dagger, and killed her. And then, with the same dagger, killed himself.

It was Benkei who found them in the little room.

"My shining lord, without your light I cannot see," he whispered.

As if to illuminate the last moments of his darkened world, Benkei set fire to the castle and threw himself into the soaring flames.